Happy tea
Sonja Sp

This book is for my daughters.

Lois, Judith and Joanna.

ZULAUF BOOKS

FIRST EDITION

First published in 2019 by Zulauf Books

Printed by Solent Design Studio Ltd

ISBN 978 1 9161771 0 9

Illustrations by Joanna Zulauf

CHAPTER 1

"Well, are you or aren't you?"

Standing by the back door, Hercules Wildside, a Bengal Tiger cat with a proud ancestry, hesitated. Why did the Insiders keep asking? Didn't they know by now he made his own decisions? Nothing to do with them. Let them wait.

Hercules raised a paw in a kind of a question mark, while his eyes pierced the darkness. He could see nothing moving but sensed a presence beyond the moonlit lawn. Usually, by this time, he would go out on what he called his 'night-time ramble' passing the goats settling down in their enclosure, then on to the hen-house where Scramble and Shelley would already be asleep. And lastly, to Muddit the guinea pig snuggling up with Rabbit. And all would be well with the world.

But tonight just felt... different. Should he venture forth? Perhaps not.

Inside activity was gathering apace in the kitchen. There were the usual reassuring sounds of pots and pans on the hob, their contents simmering away nicely. The Insiders were busy distributing cutlery on the long wooden table, And the smells. Enticing. Hard to resist.

Yes, he had decided. A good meal followed by a long nights sleep was what he needed. Then, in the morning he would sort out whatever needed to be sorted out. With these thoughts Hercules sidled through the half-open door, leaving the menacing and unsettling night well and truly out of sight; and for the moment out of mind.

CHAPTER 2

The next morning, having escaped through the kitchen door, Hercules concealed himself behind a large fern whilst he considered his options. His ears twitched, picking up sounds from around the garden and beyond. The excited chatter of blue tits at the bird table; traffic from the main road making an almost continuous hum. Far beyond the horse field, two boys were calling out to one another on their way to school. High above a plane droned its way to somewhere else.

Hercules surveyed the garden which stretched down to the gate, beyond which lay the Deep Dark Forest. The usual sights and sounds of early morning in mid-summer.

Something was wrong though. But what? This was one of the times he couldn't work things out for himself. Should he talk matters over with someone? Who would that someone be? He considered the two horses. They were out in their field most of the time and might have noticed something. Yes, he would have a word with them, and perhaps call in on the goats. Might they have some information as they were always gazing out beyond the wire fence?

Then there were the hens Scramble and Shelley; though he did wonder about them. Neither seemed to focus on anything or stay in one place for more than a moment. He had watched as time and time again they rushed about, often in different directions, then back again, almost colliding with one another. And all that scratching about in the dirt. Hercules decided they were never still for long enough to have noticed anything.

As he was considering these possibilities, Muddit the guinea pig appeared from behind the sundial on his way to his favourite clover patch. Of course. Why hadn't he thought of Muddit, who was always good for new ideas and sorting out problems? In the circumstances a useful ally. He would catch up with him before the serious eating started and find out if he had noticed anything out of the ordinary. Ah, thought Hercules, that was a good idea in itself.

CHAPTER 3

Hercules meeting up with Muddit proved somewhat unsatisfactory. It transpired he had not seen anything out of the ordinary and didn't really want to think about it. He had his own concerns to sort out. The main one being The Big Surprise.

Muddit recalled how one day, maybe it was yesterday, that the Insiders had gathered around him in a sympathetic sort of way, all talking at once.

"Muddit's looking a bit lonely don't you think?"

"He doesn't like being by himself."

"I think that's a great idea!."

But what was a great idea? They didn't explain. They just referred to it as 'The Big Surprise'.

Surprises are things that happen out of the blue. They are unexpected events in life; all sorts from everywhere. A sudden clap of thunder when the sun is still shining; the first conker of the year falling on your head; meeting friends when you thought they were elsewhere. In fact, things you hadn't foreseen. Some pleasant, some not.

But to be told in advance of a surprise. Now that can be a little unsettling. 'The Big Surprise' can very quickly become 'The Big Worry'.

Muddit couldn't make sense of it. When he came to think about it, why was he lonely? It was the Insider's fault. Hadn't they moved Rabbit indoors a few days ago with "She's a bit under the weather". She didn't seem under the weather now. There she was sitting on the conservatory windowsill, looking as bright as a button, nodding and smiling as if she knew all about everything. Anyway, indoors didn't have weather. And now Hercules was bothering him about things he might have seen, burdening him with another's problem. Enough is enough thought Muddit as he resolutely set forth to tackle a late breakfast.

Hercules went in the opposite direction, disappointed that his encounter with Muddit hadn't solved anything. Maybe something would turn up later. Nothing to worry about... yet.

CHAPTER 4

When Muddit finally stopped worrying about 'The Big Surprise' he discovered he was bored. He knew he was bored because he kept saying "I'm bored". Then he waited awhile and as nothing happened he said it again, but slightly differently "I am really bored". His brain seemed to go fuzzy just thinking about it. "Totally bored" he added as an afterthought.

Even the leaves on the apple tree seemed bored. Yesterday the wind and rain had caused them to dance merry tarantellas. They didn't stop moving. Oh, the excitement of it all. Now, today... nothing. The leaves hung there, worn out and dispirited. In fact, totally bored.

The horses in the far field seemed bored too. They had run out of interesting conversations with the goats over the wire fence. There they stood in the middle of the field not focusing on anything. Muddit could tell, even from a distance, that they were bored.

It was while he was thinking of nothing in particular, that he suddenly saw something descending over the far line of trees. A vibrato of starlings overhead distracted him, and when he looked again there was nothing there. He had only caught a glimpse and felt that if he'd been concentrating he would now know what it was. He had spotted it too late. Now, trying to make sense of it, he felt that it was something that shouldn't have been there.

So what would come floating down, yes it was floating he decided, though not like a bird coming into land.

While he had been considering what he had almost seen, Muddit, without realising it had started to make his way across the horse field towards the distant trees. It was the first time he had ventured into the field. "Nothing too daunting" he hoped, but a phrase that came into his mind "I'm in unknown territory" kept hammering away.

The grasses were coarse and cut into his sides. Thistles like angry sentinels barred his way and clusters of nettles conspired to impede his progress. But full of curiosity he continued to skirt the field. The strange thing was, the longer he kept going, the far trees didn't seem to get any nearer.

"Did you see that? What was it?" Muddit called out to the horses. They looked at him with some surprise.

"What are you talking about?" No help from them.

He was now aware that his feet had become rather sore, as he was unaccustomed to walking over stony ground. On his return he decided immersion in a mustard bath might be helpful. Or was that a remedy for a cold? It was something his grandmother had been a firm believer in. But where would he acquire the mustard? Maybe dunking a chickweed in some hot water might do the trick.

When he looked around for the horses, they were nowhere to be seen. And now there were more thistles and nettles barring his way. Muddit thought for a while. What would he do once he reached the trees? Whatever had landed might be in hiding nearby.

It now occurred to him that he could be in danger. But from what? He didn't really know what he was looking for. Would it bite him? Would it chase after him? And most importantly, would he be able to get away? He had decided he had come further than he should. "Best to turn back," he said to himself. When he turned around he could only glimpse the chimney pots of the Insider's house far away. "Oh, why did I have to go chasing after things?" An afternoon lazing about in the sun would have been preferable to the anxiety he was feeling now.

A familiar voice caused him to stop in his tracks. "You're a bit far from home" commented Hercules. He had been watching Muddit for some time and wondered why he seemed in such a great hurry. He had the demeanour of one who was running away from something. What was going on? Hercules was still experiencing the feelings of disquiet he'd had the previous evening.

Muddit didn't want to admit that he'd been scared, and maybe not mention the sore feet. Nevertheless, he was glad to see Hercules, knowing they could continue the journey back together.

"Well?" Hercules obviously wanted some sort of explanation. "Why not," thought Muddit "I'll see what he thinks about my sighting (or almost sighting)". He had to be careful in his conversations with Hercules, who had such decided views about everything. On the odd occasion when Muddit had expressed an opinion, Hercules would instantly dismiss it as being "irrelevant". How many times had he heard him say "Muddit that really is irrelevant. Get a life."

"You're limping" Hercules observed. Oh dear, thought Muddit. He had been determined not to bring sore feet and mustard baths into the conversation. He shrugged dismissively. "So what's going on?" Hercules persisted. "I'm not sure. I don't know. I caught a glimpse of something; something in the sky above the trees." Before he could get any further Hercules started bombarding him with questions

"Was it some sort of bird?"

"Well not exactly"

"Maybe a big bird coming into land?"

"I think it was too big for a bird."

"Did it have wings?"

"I really don't know"

"What colour was it? Did it make a noise?"

Muddit considered all the possibilities and didn't feel he had satisfactory answers to any of them. He was now utterly miserable, wishing he hadn't seen (or almost seen) something.

"Funny fellow," thought Hercules. "A lot of fuss and bother about nothing." And yet he couldn't quite dismiss his earlier feelings of unease.

They walked back the rest of the way in silence. By now Muddit had calmed down sufficiently to contemplate a large dandelion. Probably it all amounted to nothing and he could forget the whole incident.

But events were about to move fast.

CHAPTER 5

Midsummer in the garden, when the afternoons were long and languid, and no one had the inclination to do much, except laze about and watch the clouds drift by. A quiet time for relaxation and reflection.

Only Scramble and Shelley were on the move. For some time they had been trying to find a way from the horse field back into the garden. In one place the wire fence sagged slightly, and it was here that they were attempting to launch themselves. So far without much success.

Muddit had been watching their efforts but he must have dozed off because he was suddenly jerked awake by the most hideous squawking and clucking. They were now back in the garden, but he could see they were in a very distressed state, rushing this way and that, losing quite a lot of feathers in the process. What had happened? Muddit decided to wander over and see what all the fuss was about.

"How's it going? Everything ok?" (It obviously wasn't.) He tried to sound calm and reassuring.

"We've just seen something awful, both of us, and we were really scared, weren't we Scramble?" Shelley turned to her for confirmation, but she could only nod, unable to speak.

"Do you want to talk about it or wait until later?" Muddit suggested. He was thinking they might need time to recover and sort themselves out.

"No no. We'll tell you what we saw, then you can say what you think."

Before anyone could say anything, Hercules emerged from under a large rhubarb leaf where he'd been listening to the conversation. "So what was it then? A hairy, scary sort of thing?"

How could Hercules be so... and here Muddit was desperately trying to think of the word he needed. It was a long word, and The Three Kings suddenly came to mind. What were they bringing? Gold, frankincense, and myrrh. Ah! Got it! Incense... insensitive. But not easy to call someone insensitive, especially if that someone was Hercules. Perhaps he could put it another way.

"Look Hercules. Give them a chance. Hear them out!"

Hercules flung a rather contemptuous look in Muddit's direction, before turning back to Scramble and Shelley. "So, what do you think you saw?"

Shelley thought for a moment. “How can I describe it?” He looked towards the horse field, but whatever it was had long gone. “It was sort of black and looked a bit like a stag beetle. You know the big beetles with the complicated antennae. They never seem to move very fast. It was like one of those but much, much bigger.”

“That’s it exactly” added Scramble. She had started to recall details, which until now she had tried to forget. “This one was enormous, really enormous. It started to breathe very rapidly; we could see its sides going in and out. Then it rolled over... and died.” Scramble began to cry. She didn’t like the idea of anything dying, even if it was only a beetle.

“Is that it?”

“Look, Hercules, it’s not that straightforward. It wasn’t an ordinary beetle. It didn’t look right in some way, and it really was huge.” Shelley wasn’t sure what else he could say to convince Hercules.

“What did you do then?”

“We ran as fast as we could!” Scramble and Shelley decided there was nothing else they could say. Scramble gave Muddit a little shrug of resignation indicating she thought Hercules wasn’t taking their beetle seriously. Slowly they made their way back to the hen house.

“So what do you make of that Muddit?” Hercules was wondering if his feelings of disquiet on the doorstep had anything to do with these mysterious sightings. “Do you think you almost saw that beetle too?”

“I don’t know Hercules. As I keep saying it was only a glimpse and so far away.”

“Perhaps we should go back to the horse field and have a look round. What do you say?”

To encounter an extra large beetle alive, or preferably dead was the last thing Muddit wanted to do. If there were no more sightings why bother to do anything? Muddit was not a great one for dealing with ‘bothers’. He still had his Big Surprise / Worry to be resolved. Why add to the list?

“Sorry Hercules, I have some important matters to attend to.” Before Hercules could reply, Muddit was making a hasty retreat, quite forgetting he had a sore foot. “Oh, for a quiet life,” he thought.

But you don’t always get what you wish for.

CHAPTER 6

A day or so later and a heavy shower of rain had kept everyone under cover until the skies cleared in the late morning. With it came that wonderful sense of relief after being cooped up. Now, blue skies and sunshine meant business as usual in the garden.

However, there was a feeling of apprehension as word got around about the Beetle Sighting. Even the rats from Woodpile Mansions had called a temporary halt to their night-time excursions to the Deep Dark Forest.

Muddit had found himself scanning the skies from time to time. He had been hoping for a quiet moment. There hadn't been a lot of these recently. And now here was Hercules appearing round the corner of the house. He supposed some sort of conversation would be required.

Maybe he could tell Hercules about the dream he'd had last night. In it he was walking along a stony path with no bushes or trees to be seen. He had a feeling he was being followed, but when he tried to turn around, there was no one there. It was all very disquieting and he had woken up suddenly, with a feeling of foreboding which had persisted into the morning.

On reflection Muddit decided not to mention any of this to Hercules, as it was probably not his sort of conversation.

Seeing Muddit, Hercules decided to broach the subject of the Sightings. He had had an idea floating at the back of his mind for a while.

An idea that wouldn't be anchored down. He wasn't even sure what the idea was. It was just there ready to pop out at the appropriate moment. So far there had been no popping.

"Muddit, do you think we should do something about all this stuff? We don't really know what's going on."

"Indeed," replied Muddit, who was quite happy to leave it that way.

Hercules fixed him with an unblinking stare. Muddit could tell he needed a bit more clarification. "There haven't been any more Sightings since Scramble and Shelley, so perhaps there's no need to do anything" he suggested. "Or, ask around" he added as an afterthought.

"Hmmm. That's not exactly what I had in mind."

Muddit felt a twinge of anxiety creep over him.

"We will call a meeting." Hercules' idea had popped at last. He was beginning to see possibilities. This was going to be his Big Idea.

"How do we do that?" Muddit was completely mystified.

"Listen Muddit. Notices will be put up, informing everyone where the meeting is to be held, and when."

"But what happens next? If everyone turns up who..?"

"Who will be in charge you mean? As the meeting is my idea I will be the one in charge. I will be the Chairperson." An important role, but he decided to leave that unsaid.

"But what about me?" Muddit felt that Hercules owed him something. His "asking around" had obviously put the idea of a meeting into Hercules' mind in the first place. Hercules considered this for a moment.

"You can be the Committee."

So everything had been settled. Or had it? Muddit never felt at his best in crowds. He turned to Hercules "Couldn't just the two of us have a meeting?"

"No." Hercules was quite certain. He would have to take a firm line with Muddit. "No," he repeated. "the two of us wouldn't be a meeting. It would be a conversation."

CHAPTER 7

"We have to get everyone together somehow"

"Whatever," said Muddit. He and Hercules had found themselves in a shady corner at the far end of the garden, and were continuing their discussion of the previous day. Hercules had decided that there were important matters to attend to. It was "all systems go" as far as he was concerned.

Now it was all becoming "official" Muddit was even less inclined to be part of the action. His idea of having casual chats with either the goats or horses (Or possibly both) seemed a distant wish.

"How will everyone know about the meeting?" Muddit was hoping nobody would get to hear about it.

"Ah." That was something Hercules hadn't considered. But how to solve it?

On the spur of the moment, Muddit decided to be helpful. After all, he supposed the Committee had to pull its weight in some way. "Didn't you mention notices some time back?" Were they part of the plan Muddit wondered.

"Ah yes," Hercules had forgotten about the notices. He followed the flight of a pigeon. It landed on the roof of the house next door from where it eyed Hercules with some distrust.

"Ah yes," spoken a little louder this time while Hercules collected his thoughts. Someone had to be responsible for the notices. What about Scramble and Shelley? Surely they would be ideal for the task. they were always rushing about and could cover a lot of ground quite quickly. He considered he had shown great restraint when listening to their experience with the Beetle (either alive or dead). He could never understand why they didn't entirely trust him. OK. He sort of realised that cats and hens were not always the best of buddies. Now though, circumstances were different. A whole lot of pulling together was necessary. He would make a real effort to be nice and friendly.

So, the decision had been made. Everyone had to know about the meeting and in due course the notices would be put in strategic places around the garden. Surely that was the first thing that had to happen. Even Muddit hadn't thought of that one.

Hercules soon discovered that Scramble and Shelley were very enthusiastic about distributing the notices. However, they were full of unexpected questions which he hadn't yet thought about. When would the meeting take place and where would it be held? He considered his usual schedules. It would have to be after breakfast and before lunch. Afternoons would not be a good idea. Everyone tended to be a bit lackadaisical, especially if they'd eaten well and the sun was hot. They'd all be seeking rest in the shade and couldn't be relied on to give sensible answers to any question he might pose.

"Shall we say soon?" suggested Hercules as that would give him time to muster his thoughts.

"And where?" ventured Scramble.

"Somewhere down the bottom of the garden", he waved a paw in the direction of the far-flung flower bed. There big leafy shrubs would shield them from prying eyes (i.e. The Insiders). The last thing he wanted was a delegation from the house intent on getting everyone back to their allotted areas.

"Righty-ho" Scramble and Shelley spent the rest of the day writing the notices and putting them in place around the garden. "There, all done," said Shelley as he put the last one up by the goat's enclosure.

The goats gathered round the notice with some excitement. It was the first time they'd had their very own notice. They surveyed it in silence for a moment. What did it mean?

IMPORTANT NOTICE

SOON

Scramble and Shelley felt rather pleased that this important task had been left to them to deal with. "Mission accomplished. Now we can relax at last."

But little did Scramble know that events would leave little time for anyone to put their feet up. As they made their way across the garden, a dark cloud passed the sun. “Watch out, watch out” it seemed to warn.

CHAPTER 8

Muddit had decided to help out with the notices. It would show solidarity with Scramble and Shelley. He felt they hadn't been treated sympathetically enough by Hercules. So quite willingly he set forth with a small bundle and headed for Woodpile Mansions; the home of the rat colony.

Although he had passed by many times, there had never been a reason to call in. As he stopped in front of Woodpile Mansions, the sun disappeared behind a cloud darkening the garden. Everything became silent and watchful. A blackbird in the nearby apple tree paused in mid-song. Muddit hesitated. Where was the entrance? He searched for a door with perhaps accompanying bell or knocker to announce his presence. He was undecided what to do and almost felt like heading back home.

"Are you looking for anyone in particular?"

Muddit jumped, stretching out one leg behind him, ready for immediate retreat.

"You didn't ring the bell" the voice continued.

Muddit turned to see an elderly rat leaning against a pile of logs, swishing his tail in a menacing fashion.

"I couldn't see one" Muddit ventured.

"Look it's right in front of you!"

"What! That rusty old chain with a ring on the end? You must be joking!"

Muddit felt not so uneasy now. What an old-fashioned bunch of bananas the Woodpile folk must be to have a contraption like that.

The Old One levered himself away from the logs and moved a little closer. "Now chummy, be careful what you're saying. Get on with it. Ring the bell and tell us why you're here." He had spotted the notices Muddit was carrying. "What you got there?"

"Notices about the meeting. Would you like one?"

"Six would be more acceptable. There are a lot of us back there" the Old One swished his tail in the direction of Woodpile Mansions. "They wouldn't want to miss out. Things could get nasty if you get my drift."

Muddit wasn't sure what the Old One was going on about. As he sounded a bit threatening Muddit gave him eight. This was not going the way he had planned it. He had to think of something suitable to say which would give him the chance to leave before anything unpleasant happened. "Read the notices" he ventured. As this produced no reaction, he added somewhat more bravely "And don't be late."

Muddit started off down the path at a determined rate. Now with a safe distance between himself and the Old One, he turned "I have to see Hercules about an important matter right away. Thank you for your time." "Phew," he thought "I'm glad that's over."

CHAPTER 9

As Hercules had watched Scramble and Shelley rushing all over the garden, putting the notices in place, a tiny doubt began to niggle away. What was supposed to happen next? As Chairperson he would be expected to give advice and have a Big Plan of Action. But what would be his Big Plan of Action? For the moment it hovered just out of reach Then there was the problem of Muddit. They had often done things together, and of course, Muddit would be taking his place as The Committee. But doing what? To start with there was the matter of his name. Hercules imagined himself addressing a large expectant crowd. "As Chairperson I have much pleasure in introducing Muddit The Committee." It didn't sound important enough. Somehow 'Muddit" didn't have enough gravitas.

At this point in his musings, he spotted Muddit coming towards him, panting a bit after his encounter with the Old One. "Muddit, your name doesn't have enough gravitas."

Muddit looked at Hercules with some alarm. "Did you mention a grave? Am I going to die?"

"No, no. all I meant was that your name doesn't sound important. It doesn't really inspire confidence. Well, sorry but it doesn't. Do you think you could possibly change it?"

“To what?” Muddit was becoming increasingly anxious. He’d just about got over the grave business and now Hercules wanted him to change his name. Hercules cast his eyes to the sky as if seeking inspiration.

“What about... Marcus Aurelius?”

Muddit nearly fell backwards with surprise. “I can’t even say that myself.” He thought for a moment. “I might manage the Marcus bit, but... the other...” Here, his voice trailed off in utter misery at the thought. “Anyway” he continued “Marcus sounds a bit like Muddit. They both start with the same letter, M and have...”, he did some quick counting, “Six letters.” He looked anxiously at Hercules “So why change?”

“Hmm” was all Hercules could say.

“If I have to change my name to be on The Committee, then you ought to change your name too. So what do you think about... Hortense?”

“But Hortense is a girl’s name...”

Quickly Muddit interrupted him “Hortense starts with the same letter as Hercules...H. They both have the same number of letters... eight. Perfect.”

Hercules considered all this and glanced at Muddit. Was this some sort of joke? Muddit didn’t seem at all concerned. He was busy inspecting a large chickweed. “Whatever,” said Hercules in an affable tone “Let’s stick with Hercules and Muddit.”

“Agreed,” said Muddit.

CHAPTER 10

The Old One had retreated to his room in Woodpile Mansions and was contemplating one of the notices he'd received from Muddit. "Soon" he pondered. "When's soon?" After a while he gave up thinking about it. He had other things on his mind.

From the outside, Woodpile Mansions was a large foreboding residence, the long-time home of a flourishing rat colony. To the rear an ancient brick wall sustained little clusters of corydalis clinging to the crumbling mortar wherever they could find a foothold. Its frontage looked out on the side wall of The Insiders' house, with its door leading into the kitchen. It was the very same door, that when left open provided Hercules with his escape route.

From time to time The Insiders would take it upon themselves to remove sections of Woodpile Mansions. The logs provided material for their fires, and this, of course, happened mainly in the winter months. The logs were replaced, though not always immediately and often weeks went by before 'extensions' were added. Some of the rats found this deeply unsettling particularly the Old One. Whenever this rearrangement occurred, he would find his front door had disappeared, only to be relocated in an entirely different part of the building. A window which had served him well with sunlight often suffered the same fate. All very disconcerting. He had once put a number above the door in the hope of affording it some permanence. He quite liked the number 3, although he didn't really know why. He had carefully written the number on a piece of plywood and nailed it firmly into place. But this had not proved a sufficient deterrent. In the end, he had propped a small board next to the door proclaiming 'Gone fishing' on one side and 'Do not disturb' on the other. This could then easily be carried and placed next to the door wherever it happened to be next.

Auntie had suggested, knowing the Old One suffered from 'a touch of the rheumatics', that he should put in central heating. In the past he had been very dismissive of the idea whenever it had been discussed. "Central heating's for namby pambies. Those who can't cope with a few draughts and breezes". "Builds up the character, having to suffer a bit" he had added. Now in his later years, he was beginning to consider the possibility of installing something on a small scale. A boiler perhaps, that would service one or two radiators. Nothing more. Anyway, he was not sure how much longer he could endure the 'structural alterations' as he liked to put it.

Auntie, however, had seized these with alacrity regarding them as 'opportunities'. She had taken no time in moving into one of the new apartments declaring it a great improvement. Added to which she no longer had to live with a vague smell of mushrooms.

"You're too set in your ways" she admonished the Old One.

“Well,” he retorted “I quite like my ways. They’ve served me well, so why should I change them now. Shouldn’t be having to deal with this at my age” he grumbled.

With her new lease of life, Auntie was often to be seen in the garden, sitting under the apple tree with her knitting.

She would try and persuade anyone who lingered long enough to tackle a bit of plain and purl. In spite of her efforts, knitting remained a complete mystery to most folks, as were her little sayings that accompanied her clicking needles "Never cast a clout till May be out" and "The stars are the street lights of eternity." What did she mean by that they wondered.

Hercules came by once in a while. Auntie just knew he would never pick up a pair of needles and 'have a go'. She would look at him sorrowfully "You know Hercules, the world would be a far happier place if everyone was a knitter."

The uncertainties at Woodpile Mansions had led to the occasional impromptu meeting between Auntie and the Old One. They discussed the possibility of relocating. Some night time excursions had been put in place. The idea being to see what lay on the other side of the Deep Dark Forest, and how feasible a move might be.

CHAPTER 11

The following morning Muddit, returning from a pre-breakfast snack of clover, was pleasantly surprised to find Rabbit was back looking bright and breezy. Obviously no longer 'under the weather.'

Having brought her up to date over The Sightings and the proposed Meeting, it occurred to him that she might have some information about The Big Surprise. After all, she had been with the Insiders for the past few days. Rabbit looked a bit uncertain "Yes, I'm sure they mentioned something." She nibbled reflectively on a small piece of carrot. "Come to think of it, they did mention they would be collecting her today."

"What!" Muddit couldn't get his head round this. Suddenly his Big Surprise / Big Worry had turned into a 'Gigantic Her'. And it seemed arrival time might be any minute.

Rabbit, having polished off the carrot, smiled encouragingly at Muddit, as if she could read his thoughts. "Your New Friend could be on her way. You'll have to be nice and welcoming. What will you talk about?

At this point Rabbit decided she'd said what she had to say. More to the point she had caught the scent of new-mown grass wafting across the garden. Time to investigate. "Don't forget to introduce me" she added as she set off down the path.

But what to talk about with The New Friend? Muddit wondered. There is only so much one can say about chickweed and groundsel plants. So what then? How could Rabbit make it all look so easy, sailing through life's troubled waters like some stately Spanish Galleon. And she hadn't even bothered to say goodbye.

"Oh dear," thought Muddit "Troubles come not singly." Firstly there was his almost Sighting, followed by Scramble and Shelley with their enormous beetle (alive then possibly dead). Then Hercules becoming an impossibly important Chairman with himself as The Committee. Now, any minute The Big Surprise (New Friend) was to be on his agenda. He wanted it all to go away. With Rabbit's return, he wished to enjoy the quiet undemanding days of summer, meandering about the garden. Together they would discover fresh clover patches and the sun would shine all day.

"Where are the good times?" Muddit wondered.

But the unpleasant events in life have a habit of stubbornly staying put.

CHAPTER 12

Meanwhile, The Big Surprise had arrived. She had been transported in a cardboard box that was now placed on the Insiders kitchen floor. Wood shavings covered the bottom of the box together with a small bowl containing a snack to cover dietary requirements en route from The Pet Shop. A label had been stuck on one of the top flaps of the box. Written in large letters were the words:

THIS WAY UP. GUINEA PIG IN TRANSIT.

Someone had pushed the box into a corner to avoid the various comings and goings of the Insiders. A phone had then rung which resulted in a lot of chatter, hastily consumed cups of tea and then the sudden departure of everyone. She heard a car start up and move off. Then complete silence.

Whilst she'd been packing her overnight bag in The Pet Shop, The Big Surprise had imagined arriving at a house perhaps seeing a welcoming balloon tied to a gate post, freshly cut dandelions for her to sample. But no. Nothing.

Having waited a few minutes and deciding she was wasn't in the mood to tackle her snack, she had an uneasy feeling she wasn't alone. Her gaze wandered along the shelves, taking in the assorted tins and packets. What a lot of pasta the Insiders consumed she thought. But coming to a place where she somehow felt a large sliced white should be residing, she, became aware of a pair of eyes surveying her. Instead of a loaf, a rather big cat was crouched, watching her.

Should she say something? The cat continued to, stare. An awkward silence followed.

Hercules, from his vantage point on the shelf, was wondering why The Big Surprise had been left for him to deal with. In the circumstances the best thing he could do would be to find Muddit and let him sort it out. He eased himself down from the shelf and slid elegantly to the floor.

"I'm Hercules. Glad to see you've arrived. Long journey?" Before The Big Surprise had a chance to reply, Hercules was heading for the half-open door which in their haste the Insiders had failed to close. "Back shortly" he added, and with a swish of his tail, he was gone.

Not the best of beginnings. Totally alone. Not what she had been expecting. A tear welled up; she blinked rapidly.

"Don't start feeling sorry for yourself." In the silence she recalled her mother's words. "Get off your backside and do something." Well, she would.

But what to do? The Insiders had told her that Muddit would show her the ropes and introduce her to everyone. There was no sign of Muddit and Hercules had left in a hurry. She wasn't too bothered about Hercules; he hadn't seemed that friendly.

The first thing was somehow to get out of the box. By leaning against one of the sides and pushing, and then with a lot more pushing she managed to tip the box over. Some of the straw and most of the snack spilled out onto the kitchen floor. But The Big Surprise was free.

Through the half-open door, she could smell freshly cut grass and a lovely flowery scent she couldn't identify. This had to be The Great Outdoors.

For too long she had resided in The Pet Shop together with the animals and birds, all wanting a home and to be cared for with a chance to breathe in fresh air.

Without hesitating she was through the door tightly clutching her overnight bag. Now she was outside she paused for a moment to get her bearings.

From Woodpile Mansions the Old One noted her presence through half-closed eyes “Another of those dratted guinea pigs. No doubt she’ll be looking for Muddit.”

The Big Surprise could not believe how wonderful and utterly, utterly fantastic the outside world was. She was on the threshold of the promised garden with the sights, sounds and smells that had been talked about, and only half believed in The Pet Shop. At last she was part of it and wanting to shout out loud “I’m here. I’m here!”

CHAPTER 13

Above, the blue sky was scattered with just the right number of clouds to look interesting. Below, in their enclosure, four goats noted the progress of one small guinea pig as she made her way past the sundial and the plastic heron holding vigil at the pond's edge.

They watched as she made her way under the washing line before finally disappearing around the corner of the far flower bed.

"Why go down the zig-zag path?"

"Dunno."

"Do you think she's lost?"

"Dunno."

"Does Muddit know she's here?"

"Dunno."

"Guess she's OK then."

They shrugged and resumed the conversation they'd been having with the horses over the wire fence.

Once more The Big Surprise paused. The garden now appeared more unruly and unwelcoming. Shrubs aggressively reached out, blocking her way and in places ivy had spread along the ground in all directions and when it ran out of somewhere to go, started to invade tree trunks and branches, twisting and turning on its way ever upward.

Ahead of her the path zigged and zagged down to a gate at the far end. It seemed a long way off, and surely not the best of places for Muddit to meet and greet her.

She was only halfway along the path when a movement caught her attention. Out of the corner of her eye, she noticed something that should have been familiar but somehow wasn't.

Then she watched with growing horror as an enormous blackbird reared up, partially hidden behind a clump of nettles. A gentle breeze that in a half-hearted way had been disturbing the leaves round about, suddenly intensified. As it did the bird started pecking at the ground as if trying to extract a worm. For a moment her initial feeling of fear was overtaken by one of concern. How thin the bird was, she thought; no rounded body and plumped up feathers.

“You poor thing, you've not had breakfast today.”

Another gust of wind caused more frantic digging. Surely this was some sort of emergency. But what did one do in an emergency? She considered various options:

1. Stand still;

2. Move backwards very, very slowly;

3. Climb the nearest tree. At least one, possibly all three, could be used when confronted by a bear. But this was a bird (a very large variety). So, probably something else was required;

4. Run as fast as you can... Yes!

Before this could be put into action, sounds from the house distracted her. The Insiders were back and she could hear her name being called.

They must think she was lost. Well, she was. Why had she gone wandering off when she should have stayed put? A bad start had become a worse start, with this hideous bird behind the nettles. She turned again towards it, but it had gone. Maybe the Insiders had frightened it away. But it had looked too thin to fly. And it certainly had no feathers.

The whole incident had unsettled her. Now her pace slowed as she made her way back towards the house. She still hoped that she might find Muddit. Perhaps he would know what it was.

CHAPTER 14

Meanwhile, Muddit had found himself in the vicinity of the goat's enclosure. he wondered if he should share his concerns with them. The Big Surprise and The Committee had been chasing each other round in his brain - unresolved.

The forthcoming meeting concerned him as he wasn't exactly clear what role, that he as The Committee had to fulfil. Maybe he wouldn't have to say too much. Hopefully he'd leave that to Hercules.

"I'm lost." A small mournful voice brought him out of his reverie. There, by the sundial was surely The Big Surprise carrying, he noted, an overnight bag. This indicated someone was intending to stay.

Muddit had been a well brought up youngster. Frequently he had been reminded to “Mind your manners.” Somehow ‘please’ and ‘thank you’ had come into the equation. Neither seemed adequate in the present set of circumstances. But he decided he’d have to say something. “Can I help you?”

“Yes please. I have no idea where I am. I should have waited inside, and I did see Hercules but he was in a bit of a hurry.”

“Typical,” thought Muddit.

“By the way I’m Nicely Thank You.”

“Well so am I. In fact I’m not doing at all badly.”

“No. You’ve got it wrong. Nicely Thank You is my name... And you are?”

“I’m Muddit, but with two Ds.” At last he felt a whole lot better. The knottiness that had been lingering in his interior was gone. He felt certain that he and Nicely Thank You were going to be the best of friends.

When Muddit considered the reason that she was now a friend, it was because Rabbit with her indisposition and subsequent removal had provided a vacancy. However she had returned and this had not affected the arrival of Nicely Thank You. Of course there was room for all three of them. Muddit turned to her “I’ve got someone I’d like you to meet, someone who’ll be a good friend too.”

Nicely Thank You had started to lag behind; there was so much to take in and wonder at. She was also making sure that no big featherless bird was coming up behind them. Muddit paused for her to catch up and together they crossed the lawn. It had been some time since he had felt at peace with himself and the world. He wondered why he had worried so much. And he hadn't mentioned chickweed or groundsel plants once.

From the kitchen window, The Insiders were reassured to note their progress.

"She's found Muddit. He'll sort everything out." They retreated back to eat their pizzas and pasta and gaze intently at their mobile phones.

High in the apple tree, a blackbird sang its salute to the day, pausing to acknowledge the reply that came from the oak tree at the bottom of the garden.

CHAPTER 15

That evening Muddit, Rabbit and Nicely Thank You ("Just call me Nicely, it's so much quicker") sat companionably together. Now supper was over it gave Muddit the opportunity to get Nicely up to date with everything. When he came to the matter of the Sightings he was amazed to discover, that even on her first day she had encountered something that seemed to resemble a Sighting. She'd been reluctant to talk about it. As it was getting late Muddit didn't want them to dwell too long on unfortunate events and so turned the conversation to the forthcoming meeting; though this also could be considered an 'unfortunate event'!

Earlier, when he had broached the subject with Rabbit she hadn't shown much interest; especially when he asked if she would care to join him on The Committee. He had felt that a Committee of one was not a proper committee. She politely declined, saying she'd had enough paperwork to last a lifetime. Muddit had been surprised that paperwork might be involved, It was not an aspect he'd been aware of. Hercules had not mentioned paperwork. Maybe Nicely would join him.

"What is a Committee?" So much had happened so quickly she was beginning to feel confused. Muddit felt that a response along the lines of "I haven't a clue" was insufficient.

"We're there to make sure Hercules doesn't make too many mistakes" was his prompt reply.

CHAPTER 16

Now that Nicely had settled in, Muddit decided it was time for a conducted tour, which would give her a chance to meet everyone.

She had got off to a flying start when she discovered Rabbit too had spent some time in the STEP INSIDE PETS STORE. They both had fond memories of Mr. and Mrs. Spralling, the joint owners. Muddit found it quite difficult to prise Nicely away and tried to persuade Rabbit to join them on The Tour, but she declined. “Count me out this time; I've got things to do.”

Muddit had set forth alone on several occasions wondering what these vital activities might be. On his return he would casually enquire, and Rabbit's reply was always “Oh. Everything's done and dusted now.” When Muddit looked round everything looked exactly the same. A layer of dust which always seemed to be present remained resolutely in place.

“We won't be long” promised Muddit as he and Nicely set forth. They hadn't gone far when they spotted Hercules coming towards them and he seemed to be in a hurry. Muddit considered this as good a moment as any to inform of the changes to The Committee. “Hi

Hercules. I won't delay you, but just to let you know that Nicely has agreed to join me on The Committee."

Even as he spoke Muddit had an uncomfortable feeling that this was something The Chairperson should attend to.

Hercules looked a little taken aback. "Hmmm" was his response. "I can't stop now; important matters..." Hercules left these 'important matters' unspecified. "By the way" he added, "One of you will have to take the minutes." With that he strode purposefully away and disappeared round the corner of the house.

"Hopefully that's taken care of The Committee situation," thought Muddit. But now he was faced with the prospect of taking some minutes somewhere. Hercules had given him no information about where they were to be taken or who would be expecting them. How would they be transported? A small shopping bag or one of those pull-along trolleys perhaps? So many unanswered questions. Muddit wondered if Hercules might consider him taking seconds instead. Surely a lighter proposition. Muddit began to feel slightly dizzy. At least he had Nicely to share any burden that might come his way.

And now the conducted tour was supposed to commence. Muddit looked towards the horse field and then back to Nicely. "The horses seem a bit busy right now. Let's give them a miss." He had suddenly realised he had forgotten their names. He had known them once, a long time ago. The Insiders always referred to them as 'The Horses'. How could he introduce them if he didn't know their names?

The two horses standing motionless in the middle of the field didn't seem at all busy to Nicely. She said nothing to Muddit as she got the feeling he had things on his mind. Best to keep quiet and see what happens next.

The afternoon was disappearing fast. Soon they would be back with Rabbit and then time for supper. All very comforting. And that's exactly what Muddit needed now. A bit of comfort. Firstly, he had to do something about The Tour.

"Who's that?" Nicely was pointing to a figure sitting under the apple tree. "Oh that's Auntie. She's always somewhere in the garden, usually knitting." Muddit quite liked Auntie especially now that she had stopped trying to teach him knitting. "Some folk are not born to be knitters, and I have to say you're one of them."

"Is Auntie part of the tour?"

Muddit considered for a moment. They could meet up with Auntie. Do the introductions. tour over, and back to Rabbit. Auntie would solve the problem. "Of course she is. Follow me and we'll get it all sorted." Muddit quickened his pace with Nicely close behind.

Auntie had already heard about the new arrival from the Old One and was ready to welcome her. It wasn't long before she learnt that Nicely could already do plain knitting. “My stitches mostly stay on the needles,” said Nicely modestly.

“Well you’re halfway there my dear. When you’ve a moment I’ll show you how to do the purl sort. Then the world is your oyster!”

Nicely frowned. What were oysters to do with knitting she wondered?

“Don’t worry” Muddit whispered in her ear “It’s one of Auntie’s sayings. Forget it.”

Nicely watched as Auntie finished her row and put her needles down and smiled. “You’ll soon be doing cables like me. Put in a bit of practice and you’ll be sailing along.” “With the oysters,” thought Nicely.

A disturbance from Woodpile Mansions made them turn. “Here comes trouble; in fact double trouble” announced Auntie. “Belsize and Caledonian only come by when...” she didn’t have time to finish as Nicely interrupted:

“What strange names they have”

“I know” replied Auntie., “Usually Bel and Cal will do. Originally their families lived in the London Underground and they were named after nearby stations. Then it all got a bit too busy and crowded for their liking. Too many people always on the move; up and down escalators, along tunnels and cluttering up the platforms. In the end they had to move here for a bit of peace and quiet.”

By now Bel and Cal, two young breathless rats had arrived, both trying to speak at once.

Auntie stopped to pick up a ball of wool. “It’s the Old One. I know what’s coming next. It’s his door again.” They nodded. “He really needs some help. He’s wandering all over the place with that **DO NOT DISTURB** board tucked under an arm.” Bel pointed in the direction of Woodpile Mansions. “He says he wants his door back before bedtime” added Cal.

“Wretched Insiders” muttered Auntie. She started packing her needles and wool into a pretty floral bag which she firmly zipped up “We’ll get together for a knitting session. I won’t forget.”

“Lead the way, Bel and Cal.” She paused, leaning confidentially towards Nicely. “A bird in the hand is worth two in the bush. Now that’s a thought.” Then she was gone.

As Nicely and Muddit made their way back to Rabbit and supper, Nicely pondered on what to her was a real dilemma. The thought of holding a little bird such as a robin or chaffinch was just about manageable. But supposing the bird was a bigger sort, say a crow, an owl or even a golden eagle. That was too much to contemplate. Surely they would be more comfortable back in the bush. But not a chirpy little robin with a golden eagle, all beak and claw. Not a good combination.

They stopped for a moment to watch a robin perched on the handle of a spade left in the middle of a flower bed. “Bright little fellow isn’t he,” Muddit remarked. They watched as he jumped about, undecided where to go next.

“So much energy, even towards the end of the day” “You know, robins are very territorial.“

“What does that mean Muddit?”

“Robins guard their own patch; they don’t want to share with anyone else. You’ll get short shrift from a robin if you try and invade.”

Nicely was wondering if the big black bird she had encountered was also territorial. From now on she wouldn’t be taking any chances and go near the zig-zag path leading to the Deep Dark Forest.

CHAPTER 17

Hercules knew as he paused on the back doorstep, that it was going to be one of those difficult days when nothing seems to be going right and the world is out of kilter.

To start with the opportunity to 'escape' from the house had come later than usual. The Insiders had overslept and were consequently late putting out the rubbish. When the kitchen door was finally opened, Hercules had been hanging about far too long and was already missing a big chunk of the day.

Having snapped at Rabbit and Nicely who happened to be passing, he decided he didn't want to get involved with anyone and their doings. Since he had made himself Chairperson, everyone kept bombarding him with questions about The Meeting or The Sightings or indeed anything else that was bothering them. As he didn't have the answer to any of these, he was trying to keep a low profile. In any case the notices regarding The Meeting had now disappeared, leaving only shreds and vestiges of the originals still attached to posts around the garden. Anyone surveying them was somewhat mystified by the message. One read IMP... NOT... and another stated ...OR....NOT whilst a third proclaimed ANT... ICE... ON.

What did it all mean? The Sightings or talk of The Sightings had been deeply disturbing to many, and these notices just added to the general disquiet.

In his present state, Hercules felt whoever came his way would get a bucket-load of unpleasantness. He had to admit it. This was not a good way to be feeling. So, with one eye on the goats who were looking expectantly in his direction, he continued resolutely across the lawn.

And it was then that he came across Prunella. Pigeons were a complete enigma to Hercules. To start with he could never make out how they always managed to look so... well, rotund. There was no beating about the bush on that. The largeness of pigeons was surprising in that they spent so much time picking away at nothings - scraps that no one else could be bothered with.

Then there was the question of their heads. Hercules wondered why they would want to poke their heads forward if at the next moment they had to be shoved back. What was the point? Why not leave their heads somewhere in the middle? Out of curiosity, he had tried this manoeuvre for himself. It had resulted in a bad case of 'stiff neck,' which had lasted into the next day.

In his more selective moments, Hercules had to admit Prunella did have some good qualities. Though when he thought a bit more he could only come up with one. He was particularly partial to lying in the sun and being almost lulled to sleep by Prunella's gentle cooing from somewhere nearby. Yes, he decided, cooing was an admirable quality to possess.

But now this Prunella character was strolling about in his space as if she owned it. Well she didn't. Prunella was not too bothered about the presence of Hercules. She knew she was about to be stalked, but experience had taught her it was only a game. Nevertheless it didn't hurt to be ready for instant take off.. Just in case.

Hercules didn't want a confrontation with Prunella. All would be well as long as she kept moving forward. Looking at backs didn't present him with a problem. Backs didn't ask questions or be inclined to argue. But having a front to deal with, that was when the trouble started. However she did need sorting out, and to that end Hercules crouched down and bit by bit inched his way towards her. He had to admire the way she could launch herself without even acknowledging his presence.

Prunella now looked down at him from the safety of a high brick wall. All he could think of saying was “Don’t forget The Meeting.” But when was it? He supposed he would have to find Muddit and possibly Nicely as she now seemed to be part of The Committee and check when the meeting was to take place. Or better still have a word with Scramble and Shelley who had written the notices. Surely they would remember. He had an idea it was to be soon, though ‘soon’ could have come and gone. Would there be a meeting at all he wondered.

Now, without hesitating Hercules headed back towards the house, hoping the kitchen door would still be open. There might be time for a late breakfast. Good thinking. Everything felt better after a satisfying breakfast.

CHAPTER 18

"It's either the weather or aches and pains"

Bel turned to Cal with some astonishment, "What are you talking about?"

Bel and Cal were sheltering under the laurel bush that marked the start of the zig-zag path. A sudden squall had sent them diving for cover. Now sunshine prevailed once more. Auntie had taken up her position under the apple tree. She was peering through her glasses at a knitting pattern; a ball of wool at her side and needles poised for action. The Old One had joined her and a long conversation had ensued.

"I think he's heading for the gate to the Deep Dark Forest. Mind he doesn't spot us."

Bel and Cal held their breath until he'd disappeared round a bend in the path.

"Why's he going there?" Bel wondered.

"Search me."

Bel had been looking up through the branches of the laurel bush. They were all moving in the gentle breeze that had come along in the aftermath of the rain. Some branches were nodding their approval; others shook from side to side expressing an emphatic 'No' whilst others swithered with indecision. And yet the laurel bush resolutely remained a laurel bush, unperturbed by the uncertainness contained within.

"He's coming back." Cal nudged Bel.

"Oh. Was he just looking?"

Cal could only come up with another "Search me."

"Suppose he's gone there to shut the gate to The Deep Dark Forest."

"Why would he do that?" Cal flicked away a dandelion seed that had alighted on his nose.

"To keep everything where it should be?"

"It might make a difference" ventured Bel.

If it was left open, the branches, shoots and brambles together with the nettles would be free to creep along the zig-zag path. Saplings would rise up between the gaps in the stones. Eventually tall trees would block out the sunlight. Bit by bit The Deep Dark Forest would cover the entire garden not stopping until it reached the kitchen door. She shivered.

"Cold?" inquired Cal

"No, just thinking."

They peered out from amongst the branches and could see Auntie and the Old One once more in deep in conversation. Occasional words and phrases wafted across to them and Bel strained to hear what was being said. It wasn't long before The Old One slowly made his way back to Woodpile Mansions, leaving Auntie to her knitting.

"Night patrol. I heard that. They must be planning another night patrol."

"You think they're going to the Deep Dark Forest then?"

"Possibly Cal. They did mention doing a reconnaissance."

"Come again?"

"I'm not sure what that means. Maybe they're going to look for something."

"What would that be? Could it be something dangerous?"

"I really don't know."

"Dragons or ghosts perhaps" ventured Cal.

These were the worse things Bel could imagine. She wasn't sure what she would do if confronted by a dragon; blasting out fire and possibly smoke. Once she had come across a picture of a dragon in a book a cousin had lent her, and certainly it was breathing out a fiery flame aimed at a person dressed in a suit of armour brandishing a sword. It took up a lot of space in the book, covering two pages. Surely there wouldn't be room for it in the forest, with all those trees getting in the way. But if it was there and a tree was set alight, a sword was hardly the right implement to put out a fire.

Then there was a ghost to consider. A different matter altogether. Ghosts tended to waft along dimly lit corridors in old houses and disappear through closed doors. Or even worse, appear through closed doors. What if one was to encounter a ghost in The Deep Dark Forest? What then? Bel shivered.

"Shall we go and say hello to Auntie? She might tell us something" suggested Cal.

For a few minutes Auntie didn't speak. She was busy counting the stitches on her needle. "One hundred. Perfect. Just what I wanted."

"I thought I saw The Old One a minute ago," Cal remarked casually.

"You did. He's been on one of his ambles, making sure the gate was shut."

"Why would he do that?" ventured Bel

"He likes to check on things" was all Auntie would say.

CHAPTER 19

Shadows lengthened across the lawn as Bel and Auntie wandered off to do something or other. Cal couldn't think what as he'd only been half-listening. Looking for some knitting needles and a ball of wool perhaps.

The sun was still quite hot considering the lateness of the hour, as Cal returned to the shade of the laurel bush. He recalled how he had approached The Old One, quite recently. In the hope of being included in one of the Night Patrols. He felt ready for some sort of adventure, and surely a Night Patrol would provide that. Yes, he'd heard about The Sightings but he'd never seen one. If he was ever confronted by a big black bird or beetle he would know what to do. No big deal there.

Cal watched an ant negotiate its way round a small stone, before disappearing under a fallen leaf. He reckoned the ant was having a more exciting time than he was.

The garden was all very well, but it didn't produce challenges. Bees buzzed and that wretched Prunella was always cooing from somewhere. the Insiders would drift in and out with armfuls of washing. The horses didn't do much except gaze. Muddit was always in a hurry. Then there was Hercules. Now Cal had to admit Hercules could be a bit of a challenge.

The Old One's words were still ringing in his ears "You're a bit on the young side my lad. One day perhaps, I'll give it some consideration." Cal had retreated full of anger and disappointment all mixed up.

Cal emerged from under the laurel bush, slowly making his way back to Woodpile Mansions. He had had enough of deliberations; now there were going to be decisions. He would go with the Night Patrol next time they set forth into The Deep Dark Forest. Well not exactly with them, more behind them in a following on capacity. Keep the Patrol in sight and go where they go. Then home again, home again, jiggerty jig. One thought lingered. Should he include Bel in all of this? He had the feeling The Deep Dark Forest scared her. Well he was scared too. But he wouldn't be alone, would he? Perhaps he should include Bel. He'd catch up with her sooner or later and broach the subject.

Bel had been a bit reluctant about the idea of following the patrol into The Deep Dark Forest. After all she had yet to venture along the zig-zag path leading to the gate beyond which lay unknown territory

Cal passed The Old One sitting outside Woodpile Mansions enjoying the last of the afternoon sun. He couldn't look him in the eye. He was unaware that the opportunity he'd been seeking was going to present itself far sooner then he could have imagined.

CHAPTER 20

It was going to be a doddle. It didn't seem like a doddle now. Why had he come? Oh why was he here? Cal had happened to hear the words "All set for tonight?" as he passed two of the senior rats conversing in a corridor at Woodpile Mansions. Cal was now writhing in agony trying to keep another tendril at bay. He'd already had to extricate himself from two particularly tenacious shoots; they were everywhere; there was a positive army of them waiting to have a go. The Deep Dark Forest was proving a bit of a challenge

"It's not fair. It's just not fair." Cal gave up struggling and now sitting motionless it occurred to him how quiet The Deep Dark Forest was. So how was it, that in this total absence he could hear his name being called? "Cal." Had he imagined it? No, there it was again. He turned towards the sound and in doing so managed to release himself from the last of the tendrils.

Unsteadily he made his way towards the sound. Bel was looking at him with large questioning eyes.

"What are you doing here?"

"Oh, nothing much. Considering my options."

"Which ones?"

"Search me Bel; search me." He could tell Bel was not satisfied with that. "OK then. I'm part of the Night Patrol."

"Which part would that be?"

"The end bit; the bit at the rear."

"So, where are the other bits?"

"I guess they've gone ahead."

"So, why aren't they waiting?"

Cal shifted from one foot to another. He'd have to tell her. "When I got back this afternoon, I passed a couple of the Night patrol hanging about. I just happened to hear '... so it's all set for tonight?' They stopped talking when they saw me."

"So, who said it was OK for you to join them?"

"That's the whole point, Bel. No-one. I just decided to tag along behind when they set out. Keep the Patrol in sight and find out what they were up to."

"So, what you're saying is, the Night Patrol have no idea you're here?"

Cal slumped down on the forest floor. "No. No idea at all."

Bel was thinking rapidly. "How far ahead might they be?"

"Search me."

"We have to catch them up fast. We'll take a chance and follow our noses. Come on, get moving."

CHAPTER 21

Sometimes a path would end in a jostling of branches and vines. A decision had to be made. Where to now? Bel had the feeling they might not be moving in the same direction as the Patrol; there had been so many twists and turns.

To add to their problems, there was the matter of Cal and the holes. He kept falling into them, and that held them up every few minutes.

"Hang on Bel, I think I've hurt my back." Somewhere he couldn't reach felt decidedly tender. "That's the second hole I've been in!"

"No Cal, I make it three. Do get a move on."

Bel didn't want to admit it, but she had no idea where they were. "Stop for a moment." A noise had alerted her. "Did you hear that?" Somewhere in the darkness, a twig had snapped. The silence that followed was heavy, immense and watchful.

"Let's get away from here" whispered Cal. "There's no way we can find the Patrol. We have to get back."

Bel nodded. "Agreed. So, let's go." But which way?

"Noses" Cal suggested. "We follow our noses"

They had only gone a yard or two when another sound stopped them in their tracks.

"That was a splash. I heard a splash."

Something had dropped or perhaps been thrown into... water? They were near water!

They were unaware they had been passing a rill pursuing its way into the darker recesses of The Forest. It was flowing almost imperceptibly towards a small building situated on a mound, only to emerge from a large wooden pipe projecting from the ancient brickwork, bubbling and frothing in its release.

Beyond this, and at some time in the past a tree had fallen into the rill in such a way that its roots pointed skywards, giving them an occasional glimpse of sunlight by day and moonlight by night.

The rill was quite happy to accommodate the tree, making little detours around the fallen branches, before it gathered momentum once more.

It had not been the best of nights to be out and about, with sudden brief squalls of rain and clouds that raced across the moon, lighting up the forest floor one moment, only to plunge it into darkness the next.

It was during one of these moments of illumination that Bel became aware of something that didn't seem to fit in. She saw a movement in the water and had a glimpse of a long shiny yellow snake-like object undulating amongst the fallen branches. She felt it should be carried forward by the flow of the water. Could it be trapped, she wondered. It had to be, yes... it was... a sidewinder!

All rats have a natural fear of snakes. They are taught in childhood how to avoid them and how to recognise different types of snake. So, if it was a sidewinder, what was it doing in water? It should be in a desert. It didn't make sense to Bel. And if it did get out from amongst the branches, would it know where she was, and come slithering towards her? "Oh help," she thought.

"Did you see that Cal? Cal?"

There was no reply. Where was he? In the darkness that now prevailed, she was quite alone. Maybe the sidewinder had found him, and he'd had no time to cry out. "Cal?" She kept her voice to a whisper as she was fearful the Patrol might be nearby.

Then a burst of moonlight and there he was, a little, hunched figure by the side of the rill. "I'm coming. I'm coming" Bel raced towards him full of concern. He looked to be in pain.

"I've just been down another hole. That's the third hole. They just keep happening."

"No Cal, that's the fourth hole." Bel wondered if she should tell him about the snake. Perhaps not. He was too busy falling into holes, he wouldn't have noticed. "Did you see a White Rabbit down any of the holes?"

"What! What are you talking about?"

"Never mind. Just get a move on." Bel was beginning to lose patience.

For a moment they stood still and listened. But no sounds emerged from anywhere. The wind, which for a while had meandered its way here and there, ceased. The whole forest seemed to be holding its breath.

"Come on" Bel persisted

They could only make slow progress. Cal had developed a limp and every few minutes Bel had to extricate herself from entanglements of ivy. After a particularly demanding encounter with some tree roots she shook herself free and then right ahead and just visible in the darkness was the familiar outline of the gate.

The gate! They were back. Well, almost back.

Beyond was the quiet garden; its inhabitants sleeping still. Dawn would be coming up fast and the first birdsong would welcome the new day.

CHAPTER 22

Muddit had woken early for a reason he couldn't fathom out, except he had a vague feeling something unexpected was about to happen. But what? Now with nothing better to do he crept forth, not wanting to wake Rabbit or Nicely.

Heavy dew on the grass caused him to hesitate. He was not over keen on wetness. He'd just found a patch of clover which had robustly established itself in the lawn. But that would have to wait. He was about to head back when he became aware of two figures making their way along the zig-zag path. Cal and Bel? So, what were they doing up so early? Muddit had not been expecting company. He was never quite sure where he stood with the folk from Woodpile Mansions. This was especially so after his recent encounter with The Old One. Nevertheless, it never hurt to act friendly.

"Hello there. A bit on the early side today?"

Cal and Bel were equally surprised to encounter Muddit. At least it wasn't Hercules at the end of the path. Cal was hoping that Muddit wouldn't notice his limp, whilst Bel was doing some quick thinking. How to divert Muddit's attention away from them? "What was that meeting all about? Do you know anything, because we've forgotten."

Muddit tried to remember the last time he'd seen a notice. He thought he might have spotted one attached to the corner post of the goat's enclosure. It was more of a fragment that merely stated "IMP".

"It was all to do with those Sightings" suggested Muddit.

Before she had time to think Bel blurted out "I think I've seen a Sighting back there" she waved a paw in the direction of the Deep Dark Forest. "It was a shiny snake sort of Sighting in the water. It looked out of place and I think..." She stopped. What had she said? Muddit would certainly tell Hercules, who was bound to inform The Old One. Then what? They could be in a whole heap of trouble.

Bel became aware of Cal looking at her reproachfully. "You never said you'd seen a snake... And why did you ask me about a White Rabbit?"

Bel snapped back "Because you were too busy disappearing down holes"

Muddit decided this was a good moment to leave. He had things to do:

1. Tell Hercules about the fresh Sighting (Yes)
2. Issue new notices (Possibly)
3. Forget the whole thing (if only).

Cal and Bel continued on their way to Woodpile Mansions. High above a plane droned its way across the sky; a blackbird announced the start of the new day from the topmost branch of the apple tree. Some bees would be busy amongst the flowerbeds and soft cooings would come from the rooftop. The horses and goats would be sharing conversations across the wire fence. Scramble and Shelley would be scratching about under the washing line. A garden at peace with itself.

There was nothing to suggest that Muddit's feeling of uncertainty was to be realised rather sooner than he could have imagined.

CHAPTER 23

It is said animals can predict an earthquake before the actual occurrence.

That same morning the dew had lingered on the grass that little bit longer; a gentle mist showed no inclination to depart from the Deep Dark Forest.

The horses, for no apparent reason, had suddenly galloped to the far end of their field. There they remained, nervously pawing the ground. And waited. The goats had shown a restlessness on waking, but as they had nowhere to go, had hunkered down in their sleeping quarters. And waited. Scramble and Shelley stopped some essential scratching and hastily retreated to the hen-house. And they too waited.

Rabbit woke from an unpleasant dream about tinned carrots. And Hercules was nowhere to be seen.

Inside Woodpile Mansions, The Old One paced the floor until the tension became too much. He cautiously opened his door to check on the **DO NOT DISTURB** notice. It was still there. Not much good that was going to be he thought. A decision had to be made and made rapidly. He fussed about behind the settee before finding what he was looking for. Making his way back to the door he placed a new board in front of the old one. On it were the words, written in large black capital letters **NEIGHBOURHOOD WATCH**.

From far away the first rumble could now be heard, all the time getting louder and louder. New sounds were taking over. Chuggings, clickings and clutterings, until a cacophony of sound exploded in the vicinity of the garden waking the Insiders who rushed from their beds.

The gravel path in front of the house added its scrunchy protest as the final grinding and coughing subsided into total silence. The Old One watched from his window as a column of dark smoke arose above the side door to the garden.

At the far end of the garden Muddit and Nicely were blissfully unaware of what was about to happen. They were breakfasting on some lush groundsel plants that Muddit had only recently discovered, and which, fortunately, had been overlooked during a recent onslaught on anything of a weedy nature.

Nicely stopped eating. She felt uneasy. Then it occurred to her. The garden was extremely empty. Usually, at this time everyone was out and about. But today. Nobody. Even the blue tits were absent from the bird table.

"Muddit, where is everybody? I can't even see Scramble and..."

"Hang on a minute" Muddit interrupted, his mouth half full of groundsel. He had a feeling his earlier disquiet was about to be realised.

"I can hear something; a sort of rumble," Nicely's voice had gone up a decibel or two as she felt the ground shift slightly. "I think we're in the middle of an earthquake."

Having finished some essential chewing, Muddit was able to give Nicely his full attention. "You could put it like that. Don't worry though it's not an earthquake, although it's almost as bad as one. You'll learn to live with it."

"Live with what?"

"It's only Mr. McAdam the gardener. He drives an old dilapidated truck. That's what you can hear. Any minute now he'll come through with all his equipment."

"Equipment for what?"

"For reorganising the garden. Here he comes now!"

They watched as Mr. McAdam flung open the side door and proceeded to unload loppers, trimmers, shears, secateurs, saws and finally and with some difficulty, a motor mower

"But what are we going to do?"

Muddit gave Nicely a reassuring pat. "We have to keep out of the way for a while. So, take a look round. When we come back you won't recognise the place."

"But I love it the way it is."

Having given Nicely some reassurance a thought suddenly occurred. He'd forgotten the hedgehogs. They were sometimes a bit slow off the mark and might not have made contingency plans.

"Hang on a minute Nicely. I've got to check on something."

"Don't leave me behind. I'm coming too."

But to Nicely's dismay Muddit was heading for the zig-zag path. That was the last place she wanted to go. She looked around, half-expecting the strange blackbird to appear from behind the bushes. There was nothing there. So far so good. "Better keep up with Muddit," she thought "Safety in numbers."

Muddit had stopped beside a large brown mound consisting of leaves, twigs, grass cuttings and the general detritus from a garden that was being well looked after.

"What's that?" Nicely enquired.

"It's The Heap. It's where the hedgehogs like to be."

"You mean they live here?"

"Certainly. I've been told it's very snug and cosy."

Muddit was now standing in the middle of the zig-zag path. He called out in the loudest voice he could manage. "Hello. Anyone there?" He waited and as nothing happened, he called again "Hello in there." Silence. "That's OK then. They must have left already. They have an evacuation route that takes them somewhere else for the day. Come on Nicely. It's time we were off too. We'll pick up Rabbit on the way."

"On the way where?" Things were happening rather too fast for Nicely's liking.

"To Rabbit's cousin. She's two gardens away and used to having us there during emergencies. So, get your skates on."

As he spoke Muddit had a vision of Auntie waving a knitting needle in his direction.

CHAPTER 24

At some stage during the day Auntie, perhaps unwisely, had ventured forth to see what was going on, and in particular to check that her apple tree was still standing. It was. And underneath it sat Mr. McAdam, a cup of tea in one hand and a plate of hot buttered scones in the other.

Auntie stood in the middle of the lawn quivering with indignation. How could he take up residence under HER tree! The effrontery of the man! She consoled herself with the thought "The sharper the storm, the sooner it's over."

“Time to be on your way" muttered Auntie to herself.

Mr. McAdam finally departed having loaded his truck with cuttings, trimmings and indeed anything else he considered to be "unnecessary" in a well-maintained garden. The clunkings and clatterings gradually faded as he made his way down the road, and was gone.

The garden could now settle back and recover, knowing in time, ivy would again clamber over walks and rambling roses would reach out in all directions. The long grasses would welcome any breeze that came their way.

A blue tit was back at the bird table as a wisp of wind disturbed the leaves of the apple tree. Prunella winged her way from one rooftop to the next. Everywhere flowers hung their heads waiting for the coolness of the evening. Peace and quietness prevailed.

CHAPTER 25

On waking the following morning Cal and Bel were confronted with identical notes that had been slipped under their doors. **URGENT SEE ME NOW**, and at the bottom of the page was the Old One's signature.

Cal turned his note over in the hope that an alternative, friendlier message might appear. But it didn't. This was the first time the Old One had written to him, apart from Birthday cards. Was it something to do with the other night? How did he know? No one had seen them in the Deep Dark Forest. Yes, they had met Muddit on the way back, but he would not have had the opportunity to inform the Old One. Mr. McAdam had put paid to that.

Cal put the note in his Snakes and Ladders box, sliding it under the board. He rarely played the game nowadays. But he couldn't ignore the fact that he had been summoned. Cal sat on the side of his bed and made a decision. Shoes would have to be worn. He tried velcroing a shoe before he realised he was putting it on the wrong foot. And anyway his shoe didn't accommodate a slight swelling. In a moment of inspiration he pulled on a pair of bed socks knitted by Auntie during a particularly harsh winter.

In her room Bel was thinking "We're going to be in a whole heap of trouble," as she searched for her toothbrush. She felt clean teeth were essential if one was to be interviewed. If she couldn't think of anything to say, she would smile. And sparkle.

Cal and Bel arrived outside the Old One's door almost at the same moment.

"Do you think he knows about..?"

"What are you going to say?"

"Why are you wearing purple bed socks?"

Before they had time to address any of the questions, the door was flung open. The Old One didn't say anything as he ushered them inside with a wave of his stick.

Everything in his room was old. An old-fashioned sideboard with barley sugar legs; a threadbare rug and in one corner a grandfather clock that was older than old. The pendulum swung back and forth so slowly... tick, tock... tick, tock. The very air in the room seemed old and musty as if it had never been allowed out; lingering there to keep the Old One company.

Bel had never been in the Old One's room before, but Cal had. He remembered going with his mother when he was much younger. She and the Old One had had one of those long, boring conversations that he'd only half-listened to. Was it something to do with cucumbers?

Now the old fellow was back in his chair, which creaked every time he shifted in it. Carefully he hooked his stick over one of its arms, adjusted his spectacles and waited.

Bel glanced at Cal. In that moment she almost hated him. There he was in his stupid purple socks; they only drew attention to his feet... and suddenly she wanted to burst into tears. Everything was Cal's fault. He shouldn't have gone to the Deep Dark Forest.

Cal was wondering if Bel might speak up. But she was saying nothing and Cal had no idea what to say himself. He had a feeling if they both said nothing, they could still be in trouble.

In the ensuing silence only the rhythmic ticking of the clock could be heard.

The Old One leaned forward in his chair. "Well?" It was then that Bel knew she had to say something. She gradually recounted all that happened to them in the Deep Dark Forest, and how she had come across a possible Sighting. She decided not to mention Cal and his propensity for falling into holes.

Cal had been listening in silence whilst he watched a spider that had stopped in its tracks halfway across the floor. It knew it had been spotted. When he looked again it had gone.

Bel finished all she had to say. She hung her head "I'm sorry."

"Me too" added Cal (he had to say something). "I..." he faltered, "I mean we thought..."

"That's just the point. You didn't think. What you did was foolhardy in the extreme. The Forest is not an easy place to be in at the best of times. And there have been consequences. Agreed?"

It seemed to Cal that the Old One was taking a long hard look at his purple socks. "So what do you mean, consequences?" Cal shifted uneasily, putting one foot behind the other.

"Call them results if you like. Let me give you an example. You go for a walk and the path you are on divides. Do you take the left or right fork?"

"I'd take the left" suggested Cal.

"OK. So you take the left. You come to a field and pick some mushrooms to take home."   "But that wouldn't happen if I went right."

"Correct."

Bel was frowning.

"Suppose there are no paths; what happens to the consequences?"

The Old One closed his eyes and thought. "Let me put it this way. Consequences are what happens next. You hardly notice them. One thing follows another. It's called Life." He wondered if they'd got the picture. He noticed Cal was beginning to inch his way towards the door. "Even by doing nothing there can be consequences."

Bel drew in her breath. A memory came to her, long forgotten. The Old One's words had brought something into focus; something she would have preferred not to think about. Way back when she had lived in the Underground she had a special friend. They went everywhere together. They were inseparable. She remembered they had been standing at the end of a station platform planning what to do when a small group of rats approached. They started jeering and taunting her friend, who often wore a hat as she said her head got cold. It had a little bouncing pom-pom on top. The gang kept laughing at her "Bobble hat, bobble hat." Bel had drawn away from her friend and stood there saying nothing, then watched as with tears welling up little Bobble Hat slipped away into the tunnel. Bel never saw her again, but she later heard that her family had moved elsewhere.

And Bel had stood there and done nothing.

The Old One surveyed Cal and Bel through his pair of rimless reading glasses. "OK. What about 'look before you leap'?"

"Auntie!" Cal shouted out and they all laughed.

"Be off with you. And shut the door behind you... Quietly."

Out in the corridor they were wondering how he had found out they had been in the Deep Dark Forest. Somehow it didn't matter anymore.

Bel felt that her life, which a short while ago had been all in pieces, was coming together.

Cal was relieved to be out of the old fusty room with the Old One in his creaking rocking chair. It's not going to happen to me, he thought. I'm never going to be old like that. NEVER. NEVER. NEVER.

CHAPTER 26

The day had not got off to a good start for Cal and Bel. Hercules, on the other hand, felt things were going his way; so far at least. The back door had been left open early and after a preliminary tour of the garden he now sat in the middle of the lawn, looking round with some satisfaction. No one was bothering him with their worries and concerns and he had yet to hear of Bel's Sighting in the Forest.

Now, with nothing better to do Hercules started thinking about circles. He wasn't sure what had started this train of thought. He had always been rather fond of the shape; no sharp edges and unexpected corners. No surprises then. Walking in a circle meant you ended up where you started from.

Then again the Insider's kitchen contained so many circles; cups, saucers, plates on the long wooden table; pots and pans on the hob; the clock on the wall. And, yes, his favourite tin of Gourmet Chunks. What a splendid circle that was.

Hercules even reckoned you could count each day as a circle. After all, you start off in the morning, go through all the business of the day; hopefully have a good nights sleep. And there it is again; another day popping up and raring to go. In fact, another circle.

And didn't the earth go around the sun in a circle and even his own galaxy The Milky Way circled round, but he had the feeling this took rather a long time. Even the whole Universe might be some sort of circle. At this point it got too much for Hercules to contemplate any further. What was it Auntie said? "What goes around comes around." Now that was a very comforting thought.

And having got the important thinking out of the way Hercules could now have the rest of the day for...... He was suddenly aware that Muddit, with Nicely following along behind, was coming towards him with a determined stride. Hercules could tell, even from a distance that this exchange was not going to be of the "How are things?" "Good. And yourself?" " Mustn't grumble" "See you later then" variety. He knew he was about to be the recipient of some vital information. He briefly acknowledged Nicely and then faced Muddit.

Hercules drew himself up to his full height, reminding himself that as Chairperson he must deal efficiently and quickly with any matters that came his way.

"Fire away. I'm all ears." He listened to Muddit's rather sketchy description of Bel's (possible) encounter with a Sighting. He was inclined to think that being in the Deep Dark Forest in the middle of the night could distort events. They could even be imagined.

Nevertheless, as Chairperson, the latest Sighting would have to be thoroughly investigated New notices might have to be circulated. Maybe ones of a more robust nature than the original paper variety. A word with the Old One perhaps. Didn't he go in for boards in some way? Surely wood was more long-lasting than paper.

Yes, action would have to be taken. After all, he was Chairperson, and as such would be expected to take the matter seriously.

CHAPTER 27

Back at Woodpile Mansions the Old One having retrieved his slipper now shuffled over to the sideboard and bending down fetched out an ancient shoe box, which had faded to a pale green over time. He carefully placed it on a small table next to his chair and, having removed the lid, peered inside. It was packed tight with photos, letters, a train timetable, a couple of holiday brochures from Skegness and Blackpool. And what was one of Auntie's knitting patterns doing in there? A classic knit 'cute in cables' - suitable for experienced knitters.

Strange how hearing about Cal and Bel's adventure in the Deep Dark Forest brought back memories of his youth. The Old One sat back in his chair, pondering for a while.

It was so long ago. He and a couple of friends had taken off one day. (He couldn't have been much older than Cal and Bel were now). Anyway, they'd found themselves on a boat sailing the high seas, ending up in a port. He remembered exploring dark alleys and passageways. But where? It had to be either Rio De Janeiro or Buenos Aires. And there at the bottom of the shoe box was the answer. The Old One carefully extracted a postcard. Its message and address had faded to indistinct lines and squiggles. Unreadable. He turned the card over. On the other side was a picture of a harbour with boats moored up. And there were the words **BUENOS AIRES**. "I knew it! I knew it was Buenos Aires!"

Suppose he'd stayed; never coming back. Closing his eyes he was back in a deckchair on a sun-drenched beach, palm trees waving in the background... "Ah," he thought, a path not taken.

But now there were more immediate matters to attend to. Cal's foot for a start. The only one who knew how to deal with such emergencies had to be Auntie. She had a store cupboard stocked with pills, potions and plasters all ready to be administered at a moment's notice. Now to get Cal round to Auntie's before he took off somewhere else.

No harm though in perhaps suggesting the application of a poultice (or was it a poltergeist?) On second thoughts he might keep quiet about that.

Picking up his stick, he was surprised to hear urgent knocking at his door. "Now what?" he muttered. "No peace for the wicked today."

CHAPTER 28

Now that he had heard the news, which he didn't want to believe, the Old One had to confirm things for himself. Slowly he made his way along the corridor until he reached the "new extension" where Auntie had happily taken up residence. Why, he thought, why today when the sun is shining and all's right with the world.

The room was empty. He knew it was empty before he knocked. But knocking on a door is required even if there's no-one there to say "Come in."

A potted geranium on the doorstep had sadly wilted, its leaves crispy and brown. He lifted the pot and found the key, but it wasn't needed. When he pushed the door open he could feel the emptiness of the room, as if it had never been occupied.

The pans usually stacked on the hob had been put away. A tea towel was neatly folded over the oven rail. Two large envelopes labeled 'Knitting' and 'Recipes' lay side by side on the counter.

Slowly his eyes took in the scene and then he noticed a large paper bag in the middle of the table. Propped up against it was a sheet of paper. Peeping inside he could see a multitude of carefully knitted squares. The top one was still on its needle trailing a length of yellow wool. As he touched the bag it crackled like an autumn bonfire.

The Old One picked up the paper, adjusted his spectacles and read:

Sorry. Ran out of time. One square to finish. Sew them all together, and there's a cot blanket for the next little one that comes along. Bel will know what to do.

Auntie x.

PS: They say that taking a first step is always difficult. So, does it mean the last one will be easy? I'm about to find out.

CHAPTER 29

Muddit was undecided where to go or what to do. Rabbit and Nicely had gone to visit Rabbit's cousin (again) which meant he had some free time. Free time could quickly turn into boredom. To Muddit, boredom was to be avoided at all costs. After all, if he hadn't been bored he wouldn't have (almost) seen a Sighting. And look where that had got him.

With that in mind, he walked determinedly in one direction in the hope that someone would crop up along the way. What he hadn't expected to see was a crumpled little figure sitting crying on a log outside Woodpile Mansions. His first inclination was to slink past, hoping Bel wouldn't spot him. He felt that coping with all that sobbing was not his cup of tea. Not his cup of tea at all. On the other hand, he could go and sit with Bel until someone came along could more adequately deal with the situation. So Option Two it was.

After a minute or two Muddit decided a small discreet cough to indicate his presence might help things along a bit.

"I'm sorry Muddit," Bel managed to say between snuffles "You haven't heard then?"

"Heard what?" Muddit felt completely mystified.

"It's Auntie" Bel managed at last. "She's gone; gone away..."

Muddit shifted on the log as his rear end was becoming distinctly uncomfortable. Ah, he thought. That explains it. "Don't worry Bel. She'll sort it out when she gets back."

Bel stopped crying and looked Muddit with amazement. "Sort what out? How can she sort anything out?"

To Muddit, it was obvious. Bel had dropped some stitches off her knitting needles (wasn't it happening all the time?) On her return Auntie would sort it out. But it did seem to him a lot of upsetness over not very much. Muddit did understand upsetness. Hadn't he had a bucket load of that with his Sighting and then the Big Surprise, and not to mention Hercules and some of his proposals. Yes, he decided, a bit of sympathy wouldn't go amiss. "She'll be back soon," he said reassuringly. "She's not one to be away for long."

"Muddit, you don't realise. She's gone, gone away forever."

Bel stood up as if she wanted to finish the conversation and go somewhere else. Muddit got up too. "Let's have a walk, you can tell me things as we go." As they made their way across the lawn, a little breeze rippled through the grass indicating evening was not far away.

"You see Muddit, Auntie went away to be by herself because she knew she was going... to die." Fresh tears welled up and Bel turned away in her distress.

"How did she know?"

"She just knew her time here was over. It happens that way. She had to be alone when that time came."

"You must think back to the good times Bel. Auntie may not be with you now, but you still have those memories. You haven't really lost her if you've got those"

Voices behind them made them turn as the Old One and Cal caught them up. Bel noticed the purple bed socks were missing and Cal was no longer limping.

"Come on my friends, get your skates on, we mustn't be late." How like Auntie the Old One sounded, Bel thought. But she hadn't got any skates. The possibility of acquiring a pair seemed unlikely, even on a temporary basis. Would wellie boots do instead? Perhaps not. She associated those with wet muddy days, sloshing through numerous puddles. Never a quick way of proceeding at speed.

"Why the hurry?" Muddit wasn't entirely sure what was about to happen next. "I think we're going to say 'Goodbye' to Auntie" suggested Cal.

"Has she come back?"

There was no time for anyone to answer.

"Come on then you two," the Old One was now leading the way towards Auntie's apple tree.

CHAPTER 30

Before long the entire population of the garden had assembled. Hercules, Scramble and Shelley, Rabbit and Nicely (now returned). The goats had somehow managed to squeeze through a gap in their fence and stood at a respectful distance in order not to trample on anyone. The horses were content to view the proceedings from their field, knowing the goats would put them in the picture later on. A group of squirrels who earlier had been bouncing about in the treetops was at the edge of the lawn waiting for the latecomers. Prunella had been one of the last to arrive and had taken up her position on the roof of the Insiders house.

Muddit with the contingent from Woodpile Mansions now took their places by the apple tree and were almost immediately joined by Hercules. He felt that something important was about to happen and as Chairperson he had to ensure he was in the right place when it did. A speech would have to be delivered and it was only right and proper that he... His thoughts were interrupted by the Old One saying something.

"Sorry, what was that?"

"I was just remarking on the numbers here. Quite a turn out don't you think?"

“Yes, that is as may be. But who are they?” Hercules had just spotted a group of hedgehogs from The Heap. They had laid out a couple of blankets on the grass and were busy investigating the contents of a

picnic hamper, whilst a game of Pig in the Middle was in full progress.
“Who invited them?” Hercules glared in their direction.

“No invitations necessary. Everybody’s welcome. Auntie was a great one for informality. She would have liked it this way.” The Old One looked around “I guess we’re all here. So, who’s going to kick the boat out?”

Hercules quickly stepped forward a pace or two, cleared his throat “As Chairperson I have much pleasure...” he stopped in mid-sentence as he became aware of a commotion which was increasing in volume by the moment.

One of the younger, if not the youngest hedgehog was rushing hither and thither waving a piece of paper at anyone who looked remotely interested. Hercules could make out his words “I drawd Auntie.” There was more flapping. “Look I did drawd Auntie.”

Hercules squinted at the picture. He could see a round head with two eyes and arms (he assumed they were arms) sticking out from either side of the head. A picture of Auntie? It looked more like a turnip. But then everyone sees things in a different way.

Hercules was quickly realising that his speech (up until now his only speech) was being rather successfully hijacked and this wretched picture was being held up for his inspection.

Hercules turned to Muddit. “You’re the Committee, you do something"

Muddit saw that all eyes were now on him. He took a deep breath. “Well, young fellow I see you’ve produced a work of art. An excellent attempt, and if I may say so a rather good likeness.”

The young hedgehog held his picture up again for Hercules to inspect, as he felt it hadn’t gained sufficient attention from that quarter. Muddit now considered that something else might be required to bring the situation to a happy conclusion.

“So your name is..?”

“Hartlepool. He’s Hartlepool.” A rather harassed looking hedgehog had now arrived, clutching a black handbag in one paw, a balloon in the other. “It’s a seaside resort” and by way of explanation she extracted a small pocket atlas, “Look I can show you where it is exactly.”

Muddit could hear Hercules harrumphing away behind him. "Would it be possible... Could you..?"

"Yes of course. I'm sorry." Hartlepool was quickly led away; they could hear his mother admonishing him "I've told you before not to go bothering everyone."

"But they liked it! At least some of them did" Hartlepool's voice was raised in protest.

Muddit nudged Hercules. "I think the Old One wants to say something."

And so do I thought Hercules. But now it came to the point he was no longer sure what he was going to say. There was nothing for it. He stepped forward again "It's time for the Old One to say a few words." That at least would give him some thinking time, and then at the appropriate moment, he would deliver some well considered and worthy thoughts.

The Old One had propped his stick against the tree trunk, and for a few seconds watched a vapour trail, straight as a chalk line drawn on a board, make its way slowly from one side of the sky to the other.

"Being here today," he began "Reminds me of a story, and I know some of you have heard it before. But nevertheless, seeing a picnic in full swing, and here he gave a little smile of acknowledgment in the direction of the hedgehogs. "I recall another occasion, another picnic one in which Auntie was present. You get the picture; blankets laid out, sandwiches being consumed, drinks being passed around. As I recall a couple of youngsters were trying to launch a homemade kite and even with Auntie lending a hand, there was no chance of that happening. No wind that day" The Old One chuckled to himself. "Then the unexpected happened; a clap of thunder followed by torrential rain and the rush to get everything and everyone under cover as quickly as possible. The next day there's Scramble at Auntie's door with a muddy and battered hat."

All eyes were on Scramble who blushed at the unexpected attention she was getting but nodded as she too recalled the moment.

"Anyway Auntie was so grateful to get her hat back, she gave it a shake and said a little mud and dampness was good for the digestion. She then put her hat on, I might add, with some difficulty and declared, now that it had shrunk, that it was a far better fit than before."

Ripples of laughter followed this story, and the Old One stepped back into the shade of the apple tree, whilst others added their memories. Rabbit particularly liked the one about Auntie (and this was before she had moved to her new apartment) who had been knitting when she went to answer a knock at the door. She got up from the chair rather too quickly. Returning to the tangled mess of wool and needles residing on the floor, she gave it a glance before announcing she had just invented a new sort of stitch.

Everyone was amazed to hear how she had managed to rescue a young hedgehog (not Hartlepool) from a large flower pot sunk into the ground for watering purposes by the Insiders. By using a needle gauge, two large knitting needles (the wooden variety), a crochet hook and a ball of Aran weight wool she had soon had him out and reunited with his family.

The Old One now wanted to say a few last words. Cal had drifted off thinking about the events in the Deep Dark Forest when he became aware of the Old One mentioning Auntie and something she'd said about rains. "What was that Bel? I missed that."

"You should be listening a bit better" and Bel, with some reluctance, repeated what she had just heard. "It seems Auntie was hoping, once she had gone, that some of us would take up the reins. Do you know what she meant Cal?"

Cal frowned for a while and eventually said: "Search me." In his experience rains only came down, he'd never seen them go in any other direction. He'd never been proved wrong yet. He remained mystified. It had now become a serious worry to him. "How can you take up rains Bel?"

"Buckets," she suggested. "And maybe ladders."

But Auntie had only expected 'some' to be involved in the task. Couldn't he be exempt; he had just sustained an injury to his foot. Cal cautiously gave it a prod. Yes, it was still a bit sore.

Muddit was now judging it time to re-activate Hercules. He could see that if he didn't make his speech now, the opportunity would be lost. With this in mind, he gave him a gentle nudge with his foot. "It's your turn again I think."

"What?" This had taken Hercules unawares. His Big Speech was still at the planning stage "Oh! Oh yes of course." He felt that the afternoon had been a complete shambles. What with the hedgehogs' picnic, and that dreadful youngster causing trouble. And then all these stories about Auntie and everyone laughing. He hoped he could deliver his words with due solemnity as befitted the occasion. In his mind, there had been too much frivolity plus some unnecessary incidents. Hercules folded his arms across his chest, and breathing deeply "Friends, as Chairperson I would like to bring these proceedings to a fitting conclusion, It has befallen me..."

Here his words were brought to an abrupt halt by the most piercing scream. It was Hartlepool again. His arms were stretched upwards, his eyes on a big blue balloon, that in a moment of forgetfulness, he had released and now was floating above the treetops, then veering away westwards, and was gone.

Hercules looked at Muddit. For a moment or two he was lost for words. Muddit waited patiently as he felt Hercules was about to say something and he would be required to respond.

"How do you think my speech went?"

Muddit hesitated. "I think... I think it was splendid, an absolutely splendid speech. Couldn't have done better myself."

CHAPTER 31

Shadows were lengthening across the lawn. And above a flight of starlings was winging its way to a roosting sight beyond the horse field.

By now almost everyone had departed. Bel remained looking up at the sky and wondering where the balloon might be. She liked watching the clouds. Sometimes on quiet days it was almost impossible to tell which way they were going. Her gaze was diverted to the apple tree. All the leaves were shaking this way and that like silent bells in the light breeze of early evening. A single leaf fell, landing at her feet, its days of dancing in the sunshine now over. She carried the curled and crisp leaf gently back home and placed it under her pillow.

That night she dreamt she was sitting with Auntie. They were both knitting squares for the cot blanket. And Auntie was smiling.

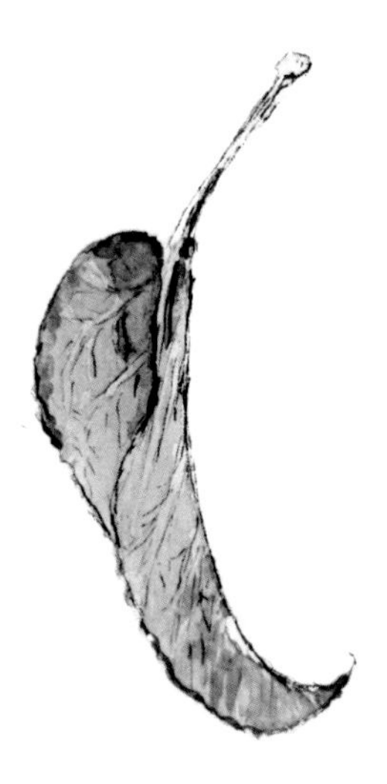

CHAPTER 32

Rabbit, Muddit and Nicely were in a reflective mood as they got ready for bed later that night.

"Do you remember that poem someone was reading?" Nicely mused. "Was it about the rain and sun and a flight of birds? Oh, and the stars."

"Yes, I remember," said Rabbit gently.

"Wasn't it saying that we are all part of something bigger? That we are never lost" Muddit added.

"I liked the bit about the stars; that they are always there for us." Nicely settled down with a contented sigh.

"Did you know," said Rabbit, "that we are all made of stardust? That's where we have come from, and that's where we will all return."

Before they slept, they looked up at the night sky twinkling with a billion, billion stars.

CHAPTER 33

"There's definitely a nip in the air" commented an Insider one morning. Sitting around the kitchen table, the others nodded in agreement, clutching mugs of tea and consuming bowls of porridge liberally sprinkled with brown sugar.

Hercules went along with that. He wasn't too bothered if the kitchen door remained firmly shut until later in the morning. Many times he had watched the skitterings of leaves racing across the lawn and noted the dewy spiders' webs festooned from every branch and post.

However, this didn't get away from the fact that he felt the need for a cat flap, giving him more flexibility in his comings and goings. Agreed, it wasn't imperative during the winter months when lingering by the log fire with one eye on the Box was more to his liking. This was especially so if a Science and Nature programme was being shown. The fact that a cat had featured in one episode caught his attention. It seemed Schrödinger had put a cat in a box (or should it have been a hat?) Anyway he wanted to find out if it was alive or dead when the box was opened. He had been kind enough to leave a sample with the cat. Hercules felt that if it was a gourmet tuna chunk the outcome looked favourable. However, a little doubt remained.

Hercules had tried to introduce the subject of Schrödinger's cat to Muddit. But Muddit considered it was not a subject he wanted to pursue for too long. However, he did wonder why Schrödinger had chosen a cat rather than a guinea pig. But considering the possible outcome for the cat, he was rather relieved.

The conversation eventually turned to other matters, and soon Hercules and Muddit were on their way.

CHAPTER 34

The Cupboard-under-the-Stairs was one of the best places to hide if you were in trouble. A place of concealment and darkness.

Over the course of time it had been used by the Insiders as a repository for

1. unwanted
2. malfunctioning
3. falling to pieces
4. might be needed later

Items. All discarded and promptly forgotten.

Hercules never ceased to be amazed by how much junk the Insiders had accumulated. Boxes (many); TVs (2); a kitchen chair minus a leg; suitcases (various); files; papers; a leaning tower of paperbacks, in danger of toppling given half a chance. A jigsaw of Brixham Harbour (1 piece missing). Propped against a wall, an ironing board in need of a new cover had recently been joined by a Hoover (minus a plug). Both now sought companionship in their later years. And there, on top of an ancient radio was the Bananagram game. Hadn't the Insiders been looking for it only last week?

The Cupboard-under-the-Stairs had cropped up in another conversation with Muddit. Muddit had found it astonishing that Hercules would want to spend time in such a place. Hercules' response had been that he needed to 'check it out' and had left it at that.

Hercules had to admit to himself that he rather enjoyed sidling along between the boxes. When he occasionally came to a dead end he would retreat out backwards, and seek a new way round. It was rather like negotiating a maze. Slightly challenging, and a whole lot of fun.

CHAPTER 35

It had to be the weekend. Hercules was certain of that. The Insiders were busy depositing bags of groceries on any available surface. The Big Shop had happened. And that only happened at weekends.

Hercules had been viewing the garden through the kitchen window. Earlier the bird table had been full of activity, and he'd caught a glimpse of Muddit heading off somewhere. That was all. Nothing to hold his interest. Nevertheless, he was waiting for the back door to be opened. His moment of release. At such times he always acted casually, as if it didn't matter whether he stayed in or ventured out. He would take his time. The matter of the cat flap remained unresolved.

In the meantime, he was prepared to sit tight keeping one eye on the garden in case something occurred that required his attention; his other eye fixed on the unpacking. He needed to ensure his provisions had been accounted for.

He was taken by surprise to find a large savoy cabbage had been placed next to him on the draining board. Then even more surprised to find a Ming Vase had joined it. (A Ming Vase!) He'd definitely heard one of the Insiders say "Careful with the Ming Vase" and everyone had laughed. Cats don't laugh. They don't even smile, except Cheshire cats.

Hercules viewed the vase with some incredulity. He'd always believed Ming Vases had been created centuries ago in China. Objects of great beauty and craftsmanship; delicate tracery of leaves and tendrils, hovering birds and benign dragons. Many of these vases are in museums, displayed protectively in glass cases and wondered at by the visitors who then move on to other antiquities. If this was a Ming Vase it was certainly not of that variety, Not at all. There it stood between the savoy cabbage and a couple of unwashed coffee mugs. To Hercules, it looked more like a jug. Its handle was embellished with a purple ribbon, and on one side was a painting of a thatched cottage at the end of a crazy paving path onto which colourful flowers overflowed. On the other side was a single rose. Had the Insiders been fobbed off Hercules wondered. A Special Offer at the supermarket (while stocks last)?

On second thoughts he might linger by the back door with the hope... But, as he turned, he brushed against the savoy cabbage, which started to roll, narrowly missing the coffee mugs, but sending the Ming Vase / Country Cottage Jug crashing to the floor.

Hercules considered it looked far more interesting in pieces, though maybe it could be reassembled with the help of some superglue. But there was no time for prolonged conjecture as he skedaddled from the kitchen; a skedaddle worthy of an Olympic Gold.

From the confines of the Cupboard-under-the-Stairs he could hear "Her...cu... leesss!" and then the sounds of china pieces being deposited in the waste bin. He knew what was going to happen next. After any disaster, minor mishap or even a tiny blip in life's arrangements "I'll put the kettle on" was to be heard.

So, for a while, he would wait in the semi-darkness until he felt it time to emerge, when, hopefully, all would be forgiven and forgotten.

And, no. Hercules had no intention of revealing to Muddit (and now possibly Nicely Thank You) the details of this particular incident. A Chairperson is an individual of some importance with a certain standing in the community, who should behave with utter propriety at all times. To tell the wider world of a possible misdemeanour was out of the question.

The next moment something happened that was to change everything.

CHAPTER 36

Someone must have opened the back door causing a gust of wind to hurtle across the kitchen, along the corridor, and as it had nowhere much else to go, blasted into the Cupboard-under- the-Stairs. Sheets of paper rose up in some confusion, eventually to settle on any available surface.

At the same time Hercules watched in horror as a white amorphous shape rose up from behind a box. It regarded him with two enormous black eyes. Hercules blinked and it was gone. What had he seen? It had only been a glimpse but something about it reminded him of a ghost. But he didn't believe in ghosts. He was a pragmatic sort of fellow, only half believing all these stories about The Sightings. Hadn't he set up a meeting and Committee with himself as Chairperson to investigate that very matter? Could he now have witnessed a Sighting and one that somehow had found its way into the Insiders house? What should he do about it? Being in the Cupboard-under- the-Stairs no longer felt like a place of safety. A refuge in a storm. He could almost hear Auntie, "Hercules you're between the devil and the deep blue sea."

Should he take a little peek around the corner of the box to satisfy himself that there was nothing there?

There are times in life when one can get lucky; when everything falls into place, and one has the answer to everything. A Bingo Moment.

Hercules was about to have his Bingo Moment, as he slowly and cautiously eased himself round the side of the box and came face to face with.... his eyes took in the scene. Now he had the answer to everything and could, at last, take decisive action. Everyone needed to know, but how was this to happen? As Hercules was considering his options a broom handle which until now had been leaning nonchalantly against the door fell into the corridor with a resounding clatter. A jittery Hercules followed with some speed (like a bat out of hell/bullet from a gun - take your pick). How comforting the seclusion of the Cupboard-under-the-Stairs had been; now he couldn't get away fast enough.

He lay sprawling on the corridor floor next to the broom handle. The Insiders looked down at him with furrowed brows "What have you done now Hercules?". It's what I'm about to do, he was thinking.

CHAPTER 37

The following day was to be the start of Hercules' Big Plan of Action. When he woke up however, he felt not very inclined to do anything. The events of the previous day had proved somewhat taxing, leaving Hercules feeling a little the worse for wear and decidedly frayed round the edges. He had a vision of Scramble and Shelley distributing yet more leaflets. He felt something of a more permanent nature was required. In the meantime, he had some vital research to attend to. Nothing too demanding, which he could do at his leisure.

Since the incident in the Cupboard-under-the-Stairs everything had changed. His own Sighting had convinced him that he was now in a position to reveal the truth. To that end, he would set up a demonstration, and this would require extremely careful planning. Weather was his prime consideration. He started to consider the sort of weather he needed. Ideally a whole lot of sunshine. A sunny day always drew the crowds and that was what he needed initially.

A light wind was his next requirement. Would that be sufficient? Something a bit stronger might be needed. A gust? Gusts tended to be accompanied by rain. How much rain? A downpour would ruin everything, causing everyone to seek cover. A few drops, over in a minute, could be coped with.

Hercules sighed as he considered these variables. Other situations seemed so easy and predictable in comparison. Go into the local Fish Bar and order two small cod and one large portion of chips (with salt and vinegar please) and that's exactly what you got. But weather. You had to take pot luck and that was that.

CHAPTER 38

With his equilibrium now restored, the day had got off to a reasonable start and Hercules was once more out and about. He hadn't gone far when a significant thought struck him. Notices! He needed notices! He turned in the direction of Woodpile Mansions with the hope that the Old One might be sitting on a log. He was. His eyes were closed and he seemed to be relishing the first warmth of the day. Hercules passed by feeling he shouldn't intrude on what was obviously a time of quiet reflection. But intrude he must.

On his return, Hercules noted one eye had opened and was regarding him with a quizzical expression.

"What's he up to now?" The Old One thought, hastily shutting his eye and hoping Hercules was off somewhere else.

But Hercules was not going anywhere. He had decided not to beat about the bush. This was not a time for niceties. "Any chance you could do me a favour?"

The Old One reluctantly opened both eyes. Hercules was up to something; he just knew it. He waited for further clarification.

"I need some boards in a hurry. A few would do. You remember the paper notices. Well more or less the same wording, though you could add the word 'demonstration' and leave out 'soon'! I suppose you've still got them" Hercules persisted. "The ones Muddit gave you way back."

The Old One was thinking. He had a vague memory of demanding a whole heap of notices from Muddit. Something to do with the Sightings. Where were they now? He had the feeling he'd treated them as junk mail and promptly binned them.

"There is some urgency in the matter." Hercules wondered if the Old One was still listening. He had shut his eyes again and was considering this request.

The Old One hadn't got much on his agenda these days. In fact, he hadn't got anything on his agenda. With Auntie gone, there was not the same motivation to get out of bed in the morning. This might be just what he needed.

"OK chummy, how soon do you want them?"

Chummy! Hercules bristled with indignation. This was not the way to address a Chairperson. In the circumstances, he reluctantly supposed he would have to overlook this indignity. He did need help.

"Make sure you mention 'demonstration' somewhere." He added, "To have the boards as soon as possible would be appreciated." And with a "Most grateful!" Hercules was on his way. He saw no point in prolonging the meeting. Maybe the back door was open. Time for a weather check.

CHAPTER 39

"He's changed his viewing habits then. I thought he rather liked that Science Programme." The Insiders were standing in the open doorway of the living room.

"He's positively glued to the screen. He hasn't noticed we're here."

What good timing they thought, always turning up at the precise moment when low troughs and spits and spots of something were being mentioned. They could never quite work out his quirks and foibles and concluded that this was another of his "funny little ways."

"Do you think he's worried about the rain? Should we issue him with an umbrella?"

"It's not an umbrella I need, it's a cat flap" Hercules brushed past them into the corridor with as much dignity as he could muster, their laughter ringing in his ear.

Giving the Insiders time to disperse to other parts of the house, Hercules returned to the living room in time to hear "The forecast is coming up in 15 minutes. I'll see you then."

You bet I'll be there. He now needed a bit more information on the weather, then it would be all systems go.

CHAPTER 40

At the precise moment Hercules was hoping for some update on the weather situation, his eyes firmly fixed on the screen, the Old One was now in his room viewing the settee with some bemusement. He'd come back full of excitement and intention. But to do what? And what was so significant about the settee? "Dratted memory, always letting me down," he thought. The trick (and he'd done this before) was to go out of the room and come back in. Hey Presto! You knew exactly what you were about.

Halfway to the door he remembered. It wasn't the settee, but rather what was behind it.

Two boards were now propped up in front of the sideboard. Only two. Had Hercules mentioned a number? Eight perhaps? The Old One didn't think so. He only had two; so two it was.

He turned, distracted by the rattling window. One of the first winds of early autumn. The weather was definitely on the turn.

He considered the boards again, weighing up the possibilities. In the end, there was only one possibility. Sandwich boards! The perfect solution. Oh, what he didn't know about sandwich boards. He'd encountered too many in his time, living in the Underground. Every time he emerged on to a pavement there was some poor fellow with boards strapped fore and aft and forced to walk up and down like some medieval form of torture. The messages they carried were somewhat similar in nature. 'Closing Down Sale'; 'Everything Must Go'; 'All at half price or less'. He feared none of that would cut the mustard as far as Hercules was concerned. But he hadn't the faintest idea what he should write.

To give himself more thinking time the Old One went in search of a tin of paint. Levering off the lid he was alarmed to see that very little paint remained and what was there had formed a thick skin. Having disposed of that he eventually found a brush (a little scrubby but just about usable) in the cutlery drawer.

He was now ready for action, but the actual words he was to write, eluded him. The small amount of remaining paint meant the message would have to be short. Extremely short.

In moments of crisis one often comes up with a solution. The Old One held the brush aloft and then quickly began to write.

CHAPTER 41

"It's a positive disaster. Look at them. How could you?"

It was some hours later and Hercules was pacing up and down in front of Auntie's apple tree. The two boards were propped up against the trunk.

The Old One was casting a critical eye over them too. Agreed. They weren't his best effort. He realised now he should have left the boards flat while the paint dried. Instead, he'd kept them upright against his sideboard. Consequently, the paint had run in black, little dribbles giving the impression that they were adverts for a horror movie

"Where is there any mention of 'demonstration'? I specifically asked for that to be included. Well? Where is it?" Hercules was now standing with his back to the boards. He could no longer bear to look at them. His Big Plan of Action was not getting off to a good start.

The Old One had never been intimidated by Hercules and he certainly wasn't going to be intimidated by him now. He'd done his best with the materials and time available. When all was said and done, a rather commendable effort.

Hercules had started to walk away full of huff and puff. The Old One waited patiently. He knew there was more to come which he felt was going to be equally unpleasant. He closed his eyes, waiting for Round Two. So, he was rather surprised to hear

"Actually, they are just what I need."

Now he'd got over the initial shock, Hercules realised that the Old One had got it spot on.

The words would intrigue, give nothing away, suggest things were about to happen. Which hopefully they were. "Good job Old One. Very well done."

Together they viewed the boards which proclaimed:

WATCH THIS SPACE.

CHAPTER 42

Hercules lingered rather longer than he had intended, listening to some rigmarole on how the boards were to be fastened and the optimum route round the garden for maximum impact. When the Old One finally departed to 'put his feet up' after the morning's exertions, Hercules was left with a problem. If the Old One thought he was going to parade here and there wedged between two boards then he had another think coming. That duty would naturally fall to the Committee. It was about time they pulled their weight. So, where were they? Hercules didn't have to wait too long until Muddit and Nicely came into view. He could tell they were off somewhere, but the somewhere would have to be put on hold.

"Ah just the folks I was looking for" he started amiably "This is of the utmost importance, and Muddit you are the only fellow who could do..."

"Do what?" Muddit was on red alert. So far he'd been rather successful in fending off Hercules' impossible demands.

For a second Hercules faltered. He hadn't entirely caught on to all that technical stuff from the Old One. Once he was launched on a subject it was difficult to stop him. Hercules finally gathered his thoughts sufficiently to say,

"How would you feel about being a sandwich... but only for today?"

Muddit stood with his mouth wide open, unable to speak.

"It's perfectly straightforward. All you have to do..."

The sound of the back door being opened stopped Hercules in mid-sentence. He needed to be back in the house for the latest weather forecast. "Oh, you can sort it out" and he was gone.

"What was that all about?" Rabbit had arrived unnoticed all brisk and business-like. "You can't possibly be a sandwich." During her recent sojourn with the Insiders she had encountered two sorts of sandwich; cheese and pickle and egg mayonnaise. In her view, Muddit had nothing to contribute to either.

"Let's get this sorted? Would anyone mind if I acquired the tapes?" Rabbit was already tugging at the two lengths that held the boards together. She had an idea she might start a plaited rug. Tape would get her off to a good start. Now for the boards. "I suggest we leave one board where it is, and if you Nicely take the other over to the goat's enclosure, it will give them something new to talk about." Rabbit had finished rolling the tapes into one neat ball. "That's that then. Anyone coming for lunch?"

CHAPTER 43

"A hurricane has been downgraded to a tropical storm and is now moving up the east coast of the United States." The weather forecaster looked decidedly cheerful at this prospect.

Hercules sitting in front of the TV glowered back. "Give me a break can't you?" He shifted slightly nearer to the screen "Get to the nitty-gritty."

For Hercules, the nitty-gritty was a forecast that would give him a sunny day, with a bit of wind thrown in from time to time. Surely not a lot to ask. Ordinary weather in fact; nothing too complicated. They could give you sun one day and wind the next. But put the two together on the same day? No such luck in that department. Oh, dear me, no. To give them their due, the forecasters were good timekeepers. "I'll be back in 15 minutes", and they were as good as their word. But now they were getting too technical for his liking. What was this talk about low troughs and dribs and drabs? Somehow Hercules associated a trough with the pig population. So how had farm animals worked their way into a weather report?

Then there was the thought of Muddit being a sandwich, running fast and loose with the Old One's boards. Anything could be happening outside. He'd done everything he could. Hopefully his Big Plan of Action was almost at the starting gate. A few loose ends to attend to, then it would be 'all systems go'.

With these thoughts, Hercules retreated behind the sofa and the next minute was dreaming of a multitude of pigs swarming all over the garden and heading straight for a trough which had been placed outside the back door (his back door). He woke up with his heart racing. A call from the kitchen summoning him to lunch did much to calm him. Maybe tomorrow might be easier to manage.

CHAPTER 44

"Where have you put the paper towels?"

"Do the grapes need washing?"

"Has anyone seen my flip flops?"

"Don't forget the frisbee"

"Where are my swimming trunks?"

There was so much activity and shouting going on in the kitchen. The Insiders were rushing in all directions. "You're in the way" they kept reminding Hercules as he manoeuvred himself from place to place. He could barely take in the conversation. But hang about; what was that about swimming trunks? He surveyed the picnic hamper, the various bags bulging with essentials. What was all this for? Of course, the Insiders were off to the seaside for the day. Hercules had a further thought. They wouldn't be going to the seaside with all that paraphernalia unless they were assured of good weather. He had missed the early morning forecast, but could this be the day he had been waiting for? The day when his Big Plan of Action, Demonstration, Sighting - call it what you will - took place. His ears pricked up, hoping for further information.

"Have you got your cardi? Might need it later."

That was it! Cardies were worn when a breeze picked up. On reflection, Hercules decided sea breezes always stayed where they were. They knew their place, so no wandering about inland. A garden breeze was another matter. He could only hope.

Now he just needed to collect his 'bits and bobs' for the Demonstration. That is how he intended to refer to them if anyone came his way and showed any interest. Everything had been hidden in a box, well to the rear of the Cupboard-under-the-Stairs. All he needed was an open back door, giving him his window of opportunity.

CHAPTER 45

Hercules was now crouched in the Cupboard-under-the-Stairs, ready to emerge to set up his Demonstration. There had been much to-ing and fro-ing in the corridor; a newspaper to be located, some last-minute washing to be pegged out. Typical of the Insiders. No advance planning or Thinking Things Through. He suddenly realised with all this activity the back door had to be open, but not for much longer. No time to delay. Split second timing was required. He encountered no one on his way to the kitchen and then with no more ado, shot through the back door almost colliding with the Old One.

The Old One had been up and about for a while. He had a nasty suspicion that some logs had been removed from Woodpile Mansions. An inspection of the building was now in progress for possible damage. He observed Hercules with some curiosity.

"You're in a hurry. Need any help with all that?"

Hercules pretended he hadn't heard. To get involved now would cause possible complications. There was no reason either to have a conversation with the goats. Glimpsing their heads poking over the wire fence, he hurried past. There was a brief wait while a retreating figure with an empty washing basket crossed the lawn. Hercules could hear the back door being shut and a key turned in the lock. The Insiders would be out of the way on a beach somewhere. Time to get everything sorted out.

CHAPTER 46

Holed up under the laurel bush, Hercules could only sit and wait. So far not a lot had been going on in the garden.

After some half-hearted scratching about Scramble and Shelley had retreated to the hen house.

Then Prunella had flapped across the garden. And that was about it.

Hercules started to consider his options. Number One on his priority list was Muddit as he was to be involved in the Demonstration. He felt all things considered he could only reveal Muddit's part in the proceedings at the very last minute. Otherwise he foresaw problems. Muddit would say he had to attend to something (chickweed, dandelions) and go charging off in the opposite direction.

Number Two was a crowd. Where do you summon a crowd from out of the blue? They are either all eager and curious, or they are not. Would two individuals constitute a crowd? Unlikely. But if something dramatic was to occur, crowds seem to gather from nowhere. "Did you see that?" "What's going on over there?" "Let's see what's happening!' And then you have it. Like magic. A crowd has materialised. Just what was required.

Something now distracted Hercules. A movement perhaps, but he couldn't locate it immediately. Then his eyes alighted on the washing line. The sleeve of one of the shirts was waving and for a moment he felt like waving back. What was causing it to wave?

Of course. A breeze had come by, unannounced, and ready to stir things up. It could be testing out what it could set in motion next time round. There were possibilities here.

So, where was Muddit?

CHAPTER 47

Rabbit, Muddit and Nicely had made a leisurely start to their day. Rabbit felt they ought to do something different. She had the feeling if they didn't seize the opportunity it might be their last chance. The weather was about to change. She felt it; something about the air (a slight coolness at the start of the day), the smell of rotting apples and the tumbling of the first leaves of autumn.

"It's going to be a bit yea and nay from now on," she announced. Then, almost to herself, "Summer days for me when every leaf is on the tree."

Eventually, all three had set forth, still with no clear objective in mind. Rabbit was optimistic, "Something will crop up sooner or later."

CHAPTER 48

Hercules was beginning to feel impatient. Big dollops of the stuff were swirling round him, and he'd started to pace up and down. He decided he needed something a little stronger than a breeze, though breezes were what he'd had in mind. Maybe if they were lined up one behind the other, each one might try to outdo the last and end by being... a gust? It looked then as if he needed gusts, but where were they?

And, where was Muddit?

Then everything happened at once. Glancing across at the washing line there were definite signs of increased movement. Two shirt sleeves were now waving, and they'd been joined by a pair of socks and a flimsy summer dress. Nearly a full orchestra.

Looking in the other direction Hercules saw Rabbit, Muddit and Nicely heading his way. He absolutely had to seize the moment. No beating about the bush. Play it casual, he told himself.

Hercules stepped forward. "Muddit I need some help. Could you grab hold of that piece of string?" He proceeded to pull a very long length of string from under the laurel bush. "There it is," he said, "All quite straightforward, nothing to it really."

Muddit hesitated. He could tell Rabbit didn't want to hang about too long and Nicely had an eye on something in the far distance. At the same time he was thinking back to other requests Hercules had made, and which he'd managed to side-step. Surely this was an entirely different matter. A simple straightforward request to hold a piece of string.

"Is this going to take very long?" Muddit inquired anxiously. Much as he wanted to be off and away, he didn't want to let Hercules down over such a trivial matter.

"No time at all Muddit. I can assure you it won't hold you up."

So, what could possibly go wrong?

Muddit took hold of the string and waited. Rabbit and Nicely were unsure whether their presence were required. Hercules noticed they were beginning to edge away.

"No, please stay. This won't take long." He needed them for crowd purposes. A small crowd of one or two was sufficient, pointing at something and getting excited. Enough to attract more onlookers.

There was now increased flapping from the washing line. Had the breeze developed into a gust? Hercules looked across at Muddit.

"Are you sure you're holding that string really tight?"

"I think so." Muddit's reply was a little dubious. How tight did Hercules mean? He was shocked into tightening his grip as Hercules' "NOW" rang in his ears.

This was the last thing he heard.

CHAPTER 49

Muddit felt himself propelled at great speed in an upward direction.

Then he stopped and had the sensation he was bobbing about like an empty drink can on a sea of waves. Gradually this movement lessened.

Muddit's eyes remained tight shut and for a while, he was unable to think about anything. "Where am I?" occurred to him at last. He was too fearful to open his eyes to find out.

He recalled how once Hercules had tried to interest him in teleportation. It seemed he had been watching some episodes of Star Trek on The Box and the characters were rather nifty at teleporting themselves to other places, often parallel universes. Hercules had expressed an interest, as he felt, once he had mastered the technique, he could then teleport himself through the back door. This would save any further discussion with the Insiders regarding his cat flap. Who would need a cat flap then?

Muddit continued to dwell on this subject. Had he been teleported somewhere? Was this a test run for Hercules' future excursions through closed doors? Another thought even more disturbing occurred to him. Had he been teleported to a parallel universe?

At this point, he decided to open his eyes. The first thing he saw was Prunella perched on the Insiders' roof. Had she been teleported too? She was regarding him with some anxiety. "How did you do that?" As he was unable to reply she continued "I wouldn't look up if I were you."

And with that, she was gone. It had been a slight consolation that Prunella was close by. He now considered the warning. Surely her advice should have been "Don't look down." Muddit felt she wouldn't know her 'left from her 'right or even more crucially her 'up' from her 'down' with all that head movement going on. The advice to "Don't look down" was given to those who, having climbed to the top of a church tower to admire the view, were overcome with giddiness and general unsteadiness. Prunella had got it all wrong and had flapped off before he could seek further guidance.

Slightly confused, Muddit decided to take a quick peep in an upward direction. Surely nothing up there but blue sky and a fluffy white cloud or two. He looked, and then wished he hadn't. Above him, but not too far above hovered the most grotesque, most shiny green and enormous frog, with a mouth that kept opening and closing, intent, it would seem on devouring Muddit at any moment.

"HELP."

He heard the word but had he uttered it; it seemed to come from somewhere else?

All he could do now was to look down. Wherever he looked was the familiar garden, the one he'd left behind. He was instantly reassured by this. As he was looking at everything from above it was difficult to be absolutely sure if this was the case. He seemed to be suspended above Auntie's apple tree. One way he could see the back of the Insider's house and close by part of Woodpile Mansions. In the other direction stretched the zig-zag path leading to the Deep Dark Forest. How would he ever return to the comforting world of the garden? Would teleporting have to be used, and would Hercules know what to do?

Everything in the garden seemed very small. It was rather reassuring to see a somewhat diminished Hercules, which could make any future encounter easier to manage. Muddit wondered what size he was, but after a few exploratory prods and pokes he decided he had remained the same. He now recalled a book he had read (possibly one Rabbit had lent him) in which Gulliver had found himself in the land of little people; the Lilliputians. But hadn't this happened after a storm? Muddit couldn't remember hearing any thunder.

He closed his eyes again and considered his options. On reflection, there didn't seem to be too many. Perhaps another glance at the scene below might not be such a bad idea.

He was rather surprised by what he saw. Everyone was standing in a line, and what was more surprising they were all holding on to his piece of string. Did they want to come up and join him? Would there be room he wondered?

And what was Rabbit saying? He could just about make out "Hold on tight". But wasn't that what he had been doing? He heard her again "Start pulling everyone".

Some jerks on the string and the next moment an unexpected encounter with the apple tree. Then he was down. Admittedly with a bump. Quite a bump in fact. Muddit consoled himself with the thought of having a cup of Rabbit's camomile tea and an early night. That would sort everything out come the morning.

"You can let go now" Rabbit's words were almost lost in the ensuing cheering and clapping. Muddit turned to Rabbit.

"Was that Hercules' speech? Have I missed it?"

"No, that was for you."

"Why, what have I done?"

Rabbit felt a slight quiver of anxiety. She wasn't at all sure what Muddit had done. She concluded that launching himself above the garden was one of his strange quirks. Nevertheless it never hurt to be considerate and encouraging. She gave him a friendly pat "Well done".

Any feeling of chipperness soon disappeared as Muddit saw Hercules striding towards him. He did not look at all pleased.

"You were meant to be ballast. And ballast always stays on the ground."

"You never mentioned ballast. I distinctly remember the word 'string' and 'hold tight' which I did."

"Hmmm" was Hercules' only reply. Things had not gone according to plan. And now he was pacing up and down in a manner that suggested he was about to demand something. So now what? Carry coals to Newcastle? Catch a falling star? Wind the bobbin up?

CHAPTER 50

But for Hercules, everything had been an utter disaster. Launching the Great Green Ghastly Frog had misfired completely. All eyes had been on Muddit. And now nobody noticed a large green plastic bag floating gently to earth beyond the apple tree.

Nobody that was except Hartlepool. He could not believe his luck. At last his very own skating rink. He skimmed across its shining surface performing toe hoops and Double Axels. He was soon joined by Scramble and Shelley who quickly discovered the Lutz and Salchows were not to their liking. Defeated they retreated to the hen house for another early night.

CHAPTER 51

Hercules became aware that the Old One was making his way towards him. He didn't look pleased, and was waving his stick about, which seemed decidedly unfriendly.

"Look here, Chummy." The Old One thumped his stick down in a very decisive way.

"What did you think you were doing? Sending that poor fellow up there. He must have been in a right state."

Hercules looked at the Old One with incredulity. He'd done it again. Chummy! How could he? But there were more important matters to attend to.

"I didn't send him up there. He just decided to go. Nothing to do with me." Hercules looked up above the apple tree as if he expected to see Muddit still there. But the Old One was expecting some explanation.

"Anyway," Hercules continued. "The only thing up there should have been my Great Green Ghastly Frog."

"Well, that takes the biscuit. Not only is that guinea pig up there, but then you dispatch a frog to join him." The Old One adjusted his glasses and glared at Hercules.

"Now that's what I call an uncharitable act. To my knowledge frogs are none too keen at being airborne." Here the Old One had to think for a moment. “In fact, they like to remain at ground level. Preferably in some damp place.”

“But don’t you see,” protested Hercules.

“It wasn’t a frog. It was a large green plastic bag.”

“Make up your mind, Chummy. Was it a bag or was it a frog?”

At the time Hercules had been rather pleased to discover the plastic bag neatly folded under an old alarm clock and a pair of gardening gloves. Exactly what he needed for his Demonstration. With a bit of judicious snipping he had cut out a large mouth. When the time came this had worked to perfection. High above the apple tree, gusts of wind had come along at precisely the right moment, causing the G.G.G.F to open and close its mouth in a very disturbing manner. Whereupon everyone would exclaim in horror “It’s another sighting”. And he, Hercules, would pull on the string to bring it back down. Upon examination they would all realise what it really was. A plastic bag. He would then embark on his Very Important Speech, pointing out that the other Sightings, manifesting themselves as a beetle, a bird or what you will were in fact plastic bags too. A simple demonstration. A straightforward explanation.

And where had these bags come from? Where else but from the Insiders. It had to be them. Hercules had seen the results of many shopping excursions. Hadn’t his tins of Gourmet Tuna Chunks arrived back home in plastic bags? Hercules sighed at the thought he now had to tackle the Insiders on yet another issue. The lack of response to his request for a cat flap did not give him much hope. Would the Insiders be ready to address the plastic bag problem?

The Old One now felt it was time to make a move. He needed to investigate the possibility of putting up shutters before the winter winds took hold.

“Can’t be dealing with all this nonsense.” He muttered to Bel and Cal.

“It’s much ado about something if Hercules has a hand in it.” Though what that “something” was, was beyond his comprehension.

CHAPTER 52

Hercules was now looking round the garden with some disquiet. It looked far from tidy; in fact, it looked dishevelled. Was that the word he needed? Oh, it would have to do. He wondered what the Insiders would make of the scuffed grass and the broken branch from the apple tree. Would they suspect him? Hardly. He felt fairly confident they would find some other explanation for the damage.

Hercules considered that his Demonstration had not convinced everyone that the Sightings were merely plastic bags like his GGGF. This was because Muddit had been the focus of attention. And now there was no opportunity to deliver his Grand Speech. This would have provided further clarification on the plastic issue. He supposed that would have to wait for the time being. A shame really as he'd gathered all the information from a Horizon programme only last Wednesday (or was it Tuesday?) It seemed there was a mighty lot of plastic floating about in the ocean as well which the fish had rather taken to. In fact, plastic seemed to be everywhere.

He wondered how fish could be so stupid. They had no discernment, with their mouths forever open, hoovering it all up. No wonder they looked so gloomy. Probably suffering from tummy ache or worse. Come to think of it, he'd never seen a happy fish. Ever.

"Is that going spare?"

Hercules was startled out of his reverie. "Have you finished with that string?" Rabbit persisted.

Hercules hadn't realised he was still clutching the last remnant. "Take it......I'm busy" "Show's over" he added somewhat tersely.

But hang on a minute. A thought had occurred to him and Rabbit might have the information he needed. It was something that happened a while back while Auntie was still around.

"Rabbit, do you remember that time Nicely found that crisp and took it to Auntie?"

Rabbit thought for a moment. Why should she respond to such a rude individual; but she did feel some sympathy for Hercules. His Demonstration had not gone according to plan.

"Yes, I know what you're talking about. I thought at the time how curious that Nicely had never encountered a crisp. Surely everyone knew about crisps. One of the Insiders must have dropped it on the grass. I remember Auntie actually pausing in her knitting and giving Nicely one of her severe looks and then..."

"Never mind about all that. Do you remember Auntie adding anything: she always did. One of her funny little sayings"

Rabbit thought for another moment "She didn't say much; just 'you are what you eat' "

Hercules was now all agog. "That's it. That's what I needed; one of Auntie's sayings. Tell me again what she said"

Rabbit sighed. She had been busy winding the string into a small ball and wanted to get back to Muddit and Nicely. She considered Muddit, in particular, needed an early night.

"You are what you eat" and with that she was gone, having spotted another length of string by the laurel bush.

Muddit had only been half listening to the conversation as he now felt a light supper and an early night would put him on the right track again. All this hanging about was not helping at all. But when he heard Rabbit recall Auntie's words, any thoughts that all was right with the world, disappeared in two shakes of a lamb's tail, or even quicker.

Muddit recalled the incident and his feeling of anxiety. What was his daily diet? He had quickly gone through the list. Groundsel and chickweed (when available). He almost forgot dandelions. So, if he turned into what he ate, there was the possibility of ending up as a dandelion, which, in the fullness of time became a clock. One o'clock, two o'clock, three...

But as nothing happened, he forgot all about it. Now out of the blue, dandelions were back on the agenda.

CHAPTER 53

Hercules, however, was still deep in thought. He was beginning to join up the dots and getting two and two to come to far more than four. Not long ago, possibly the day before yesterday he had been passing the Insider's bathroom on the top landing. He had paused in the open doorway, bewitched by what he saw within. There on the shelf above the wash basin resided three plastic fish, resplendent in carmine, aquamarine, and chartreuse. Never had Hercules seen such shimmering colours. From the end of the shelf a shiny yellow plastic duck stood like a Sergeant-Major surveying his troops "Attention. About turn. Quick March. Left right, left right" But no words were spoken, and nothing moved.

Now thinking back, and with Auntie's words recalled, it suddenly all made sense. Those plastic fish had once been real live fish swimming about devouring all the plastic that came their way. You are what you eat after all. Well, there you have it.

Hercules now wondered how this transformation had happened; overnight or little by little..... a scale here, a fin there? The Horizon programme had failed to mention this very important fact. Maybe they'd get around to it in a later series. But, the evidence was there. There on the bathroom shelf.

But what about the duck? It must have gulped down a load of plastic when it wasn't thinking. With these troubling thoughts his eyes then alighted on the heron waiting at the pond's edge. It had been there as long as he could remember. Of course; it was the plastic variety and like the fish and the duck, immovable. How could it happen to a heron; the most elegant and thoughtful of birds. Standing for so long, considering its options. Then taking flight with such careless ease.

Another worrying thought then occurred to Hercules. Might he turn to plastic by eating tuna, even the gourmet variety? The idea of sitting on the back doorstep as a plastic version of himself, surveying the cat flap (which too late the Insiders had installed) and which he could no longer enter or exit, was, too dreadful to contemplate.

Hercules tried to recall the ingredients as listed on the tin. He felt reasonably certain plastic had not been there, even as 1% at the bottom. But he wasn't entirely sure. His anxiety was rising to Level 10 on the Richter Scale. If it wasn't there before it was definitely heading that way now.

He glanced towards Rabbit, Muddit and Nicely. Rabbit was making little 'hurry up' signs for him to join them. Why not. Immediately he could tell Muddit wanted to say something.

"Hercules, the Committee, that is, Nicely and myself are resigning"

Hercules looked at him with some disfavour. What was this all about? Slipping out of their responsibilities, without a by your leave. "Hmm" What he wondered was he supposed to do about that. But wait a minute. Why hadn't he thought about it?

"Good thinking. I too am tending my resignation as Chairperson." The relief he now felt. He reckoned he was back to a more manageable Level 3 on the Richter Scale.

They walked towards the house in silence, Hercules slipping away towards the back door, when another thought came into his head. Was it last night or perhaps the night before when he'd just polished off his supper, and become aware of the mellifluous tones of Sir David Attenborough on Radio 4?

As he'd been intent on catching up with a programme on the Box, he hadn't been paying much attention. But now he was recalling something. Yes, it was all about the oceans being clogged up with PLASTIC! Why hadn't he stopped to listen? Sir David had seemed very concerned and if he was concerned he needed help.

In fact, he needed a Chairperson to run meetings, see that notices were distributed, make speeches and perhaps rustle up the occasional demonstration (though a slight question mark hung over that) Hercules decided to reinstate himself as Chairperson as quickly as possible.

But what about the Committee? He decided not to involve Muddit and Nicely as he considered their support had fallen short at times.

So why not approach Sir David Attenborough; a person held in high regard. No need for anyone else to be involved. Of course, things would have to be run rather differently; no excuses regarding chickweed or dandelions.

So that was sorted. What a team they would make. Together, he, Hercules, and Sir David, the perfect combination, would rid the world of all its plastic.

Hercules glanced towards the retreating figures. Had he been too hasty in accepting their resignation? He thought for a moment and almost instantly came up with the solution. If not Committee members maybe Muddit and Nicely would consider being a Sub-Committee. Surely not such an onerous proposition? And while he was at it Rabbit might…

His musings were brought to a sudden halt as the kitchen door was opened.

CHAPTER 54

"Well are you or aren't you?"

Standing by the backdoor, Hercules hesitated. Why did the Insiders keep asking? Didn't they know by now he made his own decisions? Nothing to do with them.

Let them wait.

THE END

Acknowledgements

John Springall. In the hope that after all those years of creativity, a little bit has now rubbed off on me.

James Oprey. For rescuing my hand-written manuscript and converting it into digital form. Without his continuing support there would be no book to read.

Mark Magee. For making all those final adjustments and fine tuning. Plus, reminding me that I haven't a clue about apostrophes.

Daniel Harvey and Imogen Harvey. For making technical adjustments, which are totally beyond my comprehension but nevertheless pleased the Illustrator.